Goliath

E. A. Briginshaw

E A Brigin
JAN 17/2014

ISBN: 978-0-9921390-0-1 (Book)
ISBN: 978-0-9921390-1-8 (eBook)

ACKNOWLEDGMENTS

Although the novel is a work of fiction, some of the characters are composite characters based on my family and friends. Thanks to all of the people who reviewed and critiqued numerous drafts of this novel including members of my family, friends, and fellow participants in the Fiction Writers' Workshop through the University of Western Ontario. Special thanks to Emily Valentini for designing the book cover.

E. A. BRIGINSHAW

*** CHAPTER 1 ***

The room was almost completely black so it was nearly impossible to see the profile of the man sitting at a desk in front of a laptop computer.

"Please enter your password:" prompted the screen as soon as the computer started.

The keys clicked as the password was entered. The password was a 24-character combination of upper and lower-case letters and numbers which made it practically impossible to crack. The person clicking the keys paused a few times as he recalled the phrase he had created to help him remember the password without writing it down. You could almost hear him hum the tune of the limerick he had created to help him remember.

When he hit the "Enter" key, the computer continued to start up. But rather than displaying the normal blue sky background and the Windows-icon used in most computers, the computer screen remained black as it continued its start-up sequence. It was obviously doing something as the lights for the hard-drive and wireless Ethernet port flashed on and off.

"Negotiating protocol...."

"Securing communications channel...."

"Welcome, Goliath" flashed on the screen, and then it scrolled down further and displayed a simple ">" prompt waiting for instructions.

"Package has been delivered," the man typed onto the keyboard.

"Waiting for further instructions," he continued.

When he entered "EOT" at the next prompt to signal the end of the transmission, the computer screen went blank and the computer shut down almost instantaneously.

*** CHAPTER 2 ***

"Attention, passengers waiting on United Airlines flight 719 from Chicago to Toronto. Your aircraft has now arrived at the terminal. After the current passengers disembark, we will be doing a quick cleanup of the aircraft before continuing on to Toronto. We expect the aircraft to be ready for boarding at gate C10 in approximately 20 minutes. We thank you for your patience."

"It looks like you guys will make it back to Toronto tonight after all," said Henry Shaw.

Henry was sitting at the airport bar with two of his workmates, Greg Blackwood and Daryl Pender. Greg was a partner with the law firm of Richards, Blackwood and Thornton, or RBT as it was more commonly known. He was tall, in his early 50's, with silver hair and had the "presence" that seemed to be a trait of successful litigators. He was always impeccably dressed, looked confident and successful - friendly, but also a little intimidating. When he was in court, witnesses were reluctant to lie or withhold information because they sensed he would eventually get the truth out of them. Even judges seemed to give added consideration to his objections.

Daryl was an associate with the firm, specializing in environmental law. He was short, in his late twenties, and anything but intimidating.

"I don't suppose you know where Gate E10 is," asked a guy sitting next to Daryl at the bar.

"You're in the wrong terminal," Daryl said. He pulled his ticket out of his suit jacket and showed the man the map of the airport on the folder. "You have to head over to Terminal 2." Daryl traced the route to Terminal 2 on the map and gave the folder to the man.

"Thanks," said the man. "This airport is massive," he said as he gathered up his belongings and headed off.

"Why is it that complete strangers always approach me for help?" Daryl asked.

"Because you look like a nice guy," Henry said. "They'd never suspect you're a lawyer."

Henry also worked for the law firm, although he wasn't a lawyer - he was the Information Technology Director. Henry was in his early 40's and had started with the firm over 15 years ago. He fit the stereotype of a computer geek as he was tall, thin and looked a little "nerdish." However, as the years passed he had put on a little weight and the recent lines in his face actually made him look better and somewhat distinguished. He had started as a computer technician and was initially involved in installing computers and fixing printers. With the growth of the firm through several mergers, his responsibility and authority within the firm had expanded. However, he knew that many of the partners still thought of him as the guy they call when the printer jams.

Another merger was the reason that Henry, Greg and Daryl were in Chicago. RBT was planning to merge with a small firm called McTavish & Company. Henry had met with McTavish's Systems Manager to plan and determine the costs of integrating their computer systems.

Daryl had come because the Chicago firm specialized in Environmental Law and was the main reason for the merger. RBT had realized that many of their clients had to deal with environmental issues both in Canada and the United States, and in some cases the laws conflicted with each other. They required an international presence to navigate these issues successfully on both sides of the border.

"I was really impressed with McTavish," Daryl said. "I've learned more about environmental law in two meetings with him than I have in the last three years of practice. I sure hope this take-over goes through."

"Merger," corrected Greg. As a partner, Greg knew the merger was pretty much a done-deal but he also knew that a political mistake like calling it a take-over could scuttle the deal quickly.

Greg headed the Technology Committee for the firm but was more than a figure-head partner on the committee. He knew enough about technology to be credible, but he was also smart enough to know when he was out of his comfort zone and dependent on the expertise of others. He had pushed several technology policies through the partnership overcoming the objections of several key partners. If Henry had tried that on his own, he would have been quickly discounted. Henry had provided Greg with all of the facts to support the recommendations and had been in the room when many of the decisions had been made. But he did not speak, nor was he asked to speak. It was during those meetings that Henry realized what a powerful ally Greg was as he overcame any objections by skillfully slicing and dicing any opposing arguments until they were left in shreds. In the end, their recommendations were normally supported by all of the partners.

Henry, Greg and Daryl had arrived in Chicago on Tuesday and were expected to be there all week working out the details of the technology plan and budget for the merged firms. Things had gone extremely well, which is why they were at the airport on Thursday night hoping to catch an earlier flight back to Toronto rather than waiting for their originally planned flight on Friday afternoon.

When they arrived at the airport, they were told that the flight was almost completely sold out. Daryl had grabbed the last seat available in economy, and Greg had upgraded his ticket to first class to get a seat. However, Henry was out of luck. There were still seats available in first class, but that option was only available to partners within the firm. It was at times like these that Henry felt the impact of the class-based hierarchy within law firms. There were partners, associates and "overhead" and he knew he fell in the last category. He could tell Greg felt bad about it, but he knew he also had to play the political game.

"Done," Greg said as he navigated a website using his phone. "You're now booked in an Executive Suite for the night at the airport hotel."

"Executive Suite?" Henry asked. "A regular room would have been fine."

Greg showed Henry his phone so he could write down the confirmation number for the reservation. Henry could see from the screen that Greg had cashed in some of his personal frequent flyer points for the upgrade to a better room. Henry was sure Greg did it somewhat to relieve his guilt about leaving him behind in Chicago, but Henry appreciated it nonetheless.

"So what do you plan to do with yourself this evening?" Daryl asked Henry as he took another sip of his drink.

"Not much," Henry said. "I'll probably just stay at the

bar and watch the game until I head to the hotel." The bar included several TV screens showing a few basketball games, a football game, and poker. It had never been clear to Henry why poker appeared on sports channels.

"Maybe you could check out some of Chicago's finest," Daryl said, gesturing with his head in the direction of two women who were sitting at a table on the other side of the bar.

Henry glanced over his right shoulder while trying not to be too conspicuous about it. Daryl was right. They were surely some of Chicago's finest looking women. One was a thin blonde wearing a black dress. She caught Henry's eye when he looked over, so he quickly looked up at one of the TV screens scattered throughout the bar. After a few seconds, he glanced over again. The other woman was a brunette in a red dress, although he couldn't quite see her as well due to the lighting. Both seemed over-dressed for an airport.

> *"Attention passengers travelling on United Airlines flight 719 to Toronto. The aircraft is now available for boarding. For those passengers travelling in first class or in rows 1 through 19, please proceed to gate C10. Please have your boarding pass and identification available for inspection at the gate. We apologize for the delay and thank you for your patience."*

"OK, let's go," Greg said. Greg and Daryl gulped down the last of their drinks and quickly gathered up their coats and suitcases. They travelled a lot so knew how to pack to fit all of their stuff into a single carry-on bag with wheels. They didn't want to waste time waiting for checked baggage.

"See you on Monday," Daryl said as they headed off.

Henry turned his focus back to the TV screens above the bar. He wasn't too interested in the basketball games but he normally followed the NFL, so switched his focus to that TV. However, that game was a blowout with New England up 48 to 10. Where the Monday night football games were normally quite close, the introduction of more Thursday night NFL games had been a disappointment. This wasn't the first time one of the Thursday night games had been one-sided.

Henry glanced over his right shoulder again and made eye contact with the blonde woman in the black dress. She smiled. Henry noticed that the other woman was nowhere to be seen. He felt someone touch him on his left elbow and turned to see that the brunette woman in the red dress had quietly slipped onto the bar stool where Daryl had been sitting.

"Hi," she said. "I'm Tammy. I was wondering if you wanted to spend the night together."

Henry couldn't speak. This woman was so beautiful that he literally stopped breathing. He knew he was blushing but he was sure he would soon turn blue due to lack of oxygen. It was only when he looked away and back at the TV screen that he started to regain his composure. He was normally very quick-witted, but his mind was racing and he couldn't seem to control it. When he finally took a breath, he started to think things through. Logic seemed to kick in again and he realized this woman was probably a hooker.

"Sorry," he said. "I'm not interested in an escort tonight." It was only then that he could turn his head to look at her again.

"I'm not a hooker," she said. She was looking him straight in the eye and he sensed she wasn't lying.

"What? No dinner, no movie, just straight to bed?" Henry felt his wittiness returning.

"You know, this usually works out better if I play the role of the woman and you play the role of the man, but if I need to buy you dinner to get you to put out, then I'm game," she said flirting with him.

Henry just stared at her for what seemed an eternity. He was trying to figure out what was going on. Maybe one of his friends was going to suddenly appear to tell him this was a practical joke, but no one knew him here in Chicago. Maybe she was a con artist and he was going to find himself mugged at the end of the night with the police asking him how he could have been so stupid.

Tammy broke the silence. "You're not married are you? Because I don't screw around with married men. You're not wearing a ring, but that doesn't mean anything these days." Suddenly it seemed like it was Tammy who was wondering what she was doing. "I'm sorry, this was a mistake. I shouldn't have done it." She glanced over at the blonde woman who had been watching the whole thing. Tammy looked embarrassed and started to slide off the bar stool to leave.

"Hi, I'm Henry," he said, holding out his hand. "Nice to meet you. No, I'm not married. So, can I buy you dinner?"

Tammy stopped her retreat. She smiled and shook his hand. "Yes, I think I would enjoy that very much. Just a second, I have to let my friend know what's going on." Tammy walked over to the blonde woman in the black dress and spoke briefly to her. They both looked over at Henry and smiled, although the blonde woman looked more worried than happy.

"Let's go," Tammy said when she returned.

Henry and Tammy walked slowly through the airport concourse. Or it seemed slow compared to the hundreds of people who seemed to be racing to catch their plane or to get out of the airport and home to their families. Many of the passengers seemed frustrated as they tried to navigate around Henry and Tammy without colliding into other people racing in the other direction. A few people mumbled obscenities and gave them dirty looks as they passed. Henry was oblivious to them.

"So where would you like to eat?" Henry asked.

"It doesn't matter," Tammy replied. "I think our choices will be somewhat limited at the airport."

They continued to saunter through the airport concourse, smiling at each other, but hardly talking. It seemed like both of them were in uncharted waters and neither of them knew what to say or do next.

They came across a restaurant/bar that looked somewhat promising. It had a sign out front that showed their menu which seemed more comprehensive than the fast food places they had passed by, although it seemed to focus on their "breakfast available all day" items. The restaurant wasn't that busy so they easily found a table. When the waitress arrived, she asked whether they wanted drinks or a full meal.

"Both," Henry said. He nodded to Tammy to let her make her choice.

"I'll have a glass of white wine and a Caesar salad," Tammy said.

"I'll have the steak sandwich and a Bacardi and Coke," Henry said. He would have normally just said a rum and coke but he felt asking for a Bacardi somehow made him seem more sophisticated. For some reason, appearing more sophisticated seemed important to him.

The waitress brought their drinks and they continued to talk while they sipped them, but they had run out of small talk and the pauses in the conversation seemed to be getting longer and longer. They were both pleased when the waitress brought their meals.

Henry had noticed that her purse had a large "*LW*" button on the clasp which made him suspicious that

Tammy wasn't her real name. "So is Tammy your real name?"

Tammy blushed with embarrassment. "No, it's actually the name of my cat. I'm not sure I want to tell you my real name, and I can't tell you why. This must seem so strange to you."

That was an understatement, although she seemed like a puzzle he wanted to solve. "Well, in the interests of full disclosure, Henry is my real name and I hate cats."

"I know - that Henry is your real name, that is, not that you hate cats. We overheard you talking with your friends at the bar. We knew you couldn't get a flight to Toronto tonight and your friends bailed on you."

"Don't they have laws against stalking here in Chicago?" Henry asked, smirking as he said it.

Tammy paused before answering, as if she was trying to navigate her way to a place she'd never been before. "Why, are you planning to have me arrested?"

"Jury's still out on that one."

"Lawyers," she said. "You know what they say. If you laid all of the lawyers end to end at the bottom of the ocean…"

"It would be a good thing," Henry said, finishing the punch-line. "But I'm not a lawyer. I just work for them. Can I ask what you do for a living?"

"Let's just say I'm in media and leave it at that."

Henry pondered her answer for a moment. "Media - that's a fairly broad category, although you're certainly pretty enough to be on TV or be a movie star," Henry said, fishing for clarification.

"Thank you, although you're going down the wrong path. I do more research than anything else."

Henry became even more intrigued, and nervous. Had he somehow become a research project about how easy it is to pick up guys in airports? How gullible guys become when they see a pretty face? He didn't like where his line of thinking was heading.

"Can I get you anything else?" asked the waitress, thankfully interrupting his train of thought.

"No, I think we're good," Henry said, glancing at Tammy for confirmation. "Just the bill please."

The waitress produced it immediately and Henry picked it up just as quickly. "I guess I'm more comfortable playing the role of the man in this relationship after all," Henry said after the waitress walked away, referring to their previous conversation about who would be paying for dinner.

They gathered their things and started out of the restaurant. Henry noticed the blonde woman in the black dress hovering at a newsstand across the concourse. She had obviously followed them.

"It looks like your friend is keeping an eye on us," Henry said.

It seemed to catch Tammy by surprise. "Oh Sam," she mumbled to herself. "I told her everything was OK. Give me a second."

Tammy crossed the concourse and spoke to her friend. Again, they both looked over at Henry smiling, but her friend's smile couldn't mask the concern on her face.

"So, your friend Sam looked a little concerned," Henry said when she returned.

Tammy stopped. "How did you..." she started to say, but then caught herself.

"You mentioned her name when we were coming out of the restaurant. I'm assuming that's short for Samantha and that it's her real name."

"It doesn't matter. We won't be running into her again."

Greg had made a reservation for Henry at the hotel that was connected to the airport, so Henry and Tammy could easily walk to it using the airport concourse. When they reached the hotel lobby, Henry went to the reception desk to check-in while Tammy wandered into the small store that sold magazines, newspapers and drinks.

"Do you have a reservation?" asked the clerk as he saw Henry approaching.

"Yes, it's under the name of Shaw."

"Here it is," said the clerk. "One night - Executive Suite - Party of one." He said the last part more as a question than a statement because he had noticed Tammy watching them while pretending to browse through the magazine stand across the lobby.

"Yes, just myself," Henry said. The female clerk at the next station shot Henry a dirty look, but then turned away as one of the lights on the phone started flashing.

"Excellent," said the male clerk. "Check-out time is noon, although we can store luggage in our back room if your flight isn't until later in the day."

"That won't be necessary. Thanks."

Henry turned towards the magazine store where Tammy had been waiting. He didn't see her so he started walking toward the elevators scanning the lobby looking for her as he went. When he got to the bank of elevators, Tammy peered out from one of them.

"Going up, sir?"

"Absolutely."

When they got to the room, Henry inserted his key-card and was surprised at how large the room was when they walked in. The room had a huge king-sized bed and a separate area with a desk, a couch and a big-screen TV. He wasn't used to this type of extravagance. He'd have to remember to thank Greg again for the upgrade when he got back to Toronto.

"Give me a few minutes to freshen up," Tammy said as

she headed towards the bathroom.

"Take your time."

When he saw the door close, Henry started turning on and off various lights in the room trying to find the right balance for romantic lighting. He started to take off his clothes, but then wasn't sure if he should, so started to put them back on again. He had no idea whether Tammy was going to emerge from the bathroom fully clothed or totally naked. He decided he'd go half-way. He took off his shirt but kept his pants on and lay on the bed on top of the covers. He still felt awkward and felt like he was trying to impersonate Bert Reynolds from an old movie he once saw. He took off his pants and slid under the covers wearing just his boxers. He turned down the covers half-way on the other side of the bed trying to create an inviting look. The room suddenly seemed way too bright so he jumped out of bed again and started turning off more and more lights so that the only remaining one was the overhead light way over by the door. He could hear the knob on the bathroom door start to turn so he raced back and dove into the bed covering the lower part of his body with the sheet.

Tammy emerged from the bathroom, fully clothed. Awkward, he thought. This reminded him of the first time he tried to seduce a girl back in high school. It didn't end well. In that case, he had suggested a midnight swim with a girl he was interested in at a summer camp. They had both gone behind some bushes to take off their clothes. He had emerged from the bushes totally naked thinking they were going skinny-dipping and she had emerged wearing a one-piece bathing suit. She called him a pervert and had raced off. It had taken him years to recover from that embarrassment, or maybe he still hadn't fully recovered from it.

Tammy didn't seem fazed or surprised at all. "It's

awfully dark in here," she said. "Mind if I turn on some lights?" She didn't wait for a response and proceeded to turn on a reading light over her side of the bed and a floor lamp near the desk.

She hiked up her red dress almost to her waist which revealed the top of her stockings. Henry wondered how they stayed up without a garter belt, although he wasn't up to speed on the engineering of women's lingerie. She put one leg up on the desk chair and slowly rolled the stocking down until it loosened and then removed it completely and draped it over the back of the chair. She repeated the procedure with the other stocking. Tammy walked over and sat on the edge of the bed with her back towards Henry. "Could you be a sweetie and unzip me?"

Henry could hardly feel his fingers but did manage to unzip her dress down to the small of her back. Her bare back revealed that she wasn't wearing a bra. Tammy stood and faced Henry. She raised her arms above her head and the red dress slowly fell to the floor.

"It must be a little cold in here," she said as she cupped her breasts. They were enormous and stood at full attention. She paused and let Henry enjoy the view. Henry reached up to fondle her breasts and she seemed to enjoy this as much as he did as she guided his hands over every inch of them.

She turned her back to him and removed her panties and let them slide down to the floor. She then grabbed them with the toes of her right leg and flicked them perfectly so they landed on the chair with her stockings. She turned and faced Henry and ran her fingers through her hair. Henry was sure he was going to lose it. Tammy approached the bed and threw back the sheet that was covering Henry's lower half, revealing the boxer shorts. "That won't do," Tammy said. She proceeded to remove Henry's shorts like a magician who pulls a table-cloth from a table without moving any of the dishes.

"Impressive," Tammy said as she observed her newly discovered toy which was reaching to the sky to meet her. She climbed onto the bed straddling Henry as she did so and slowly slid down on top of him.

"Oh God, Oh God," Henry moaned as he came almost immediately. "I'm sorry. I didn't mean to," Henry said. "I'm so sorry," he kept repeating.

"No you're not," Tammy said, looking down at him. Rather than looking disappointed, she looked totally pleased with herself. "But you owe me and you'll have to make it up to me."

And he did. Three more times that night.

* * *

Henry awoke the next morning to the sound of the shower coming from the bathroom. He could hear Tammy singing, but he couldn't quite make out the tune. He couldn't remember the last time he'd had such a night of passion. He heard the shower stop and sat up in bed anticipating Tammy's return. He glanced over at the clock on the table beside the bed and saw that it was just after 11AM.

Tammy emerged from the bathroom wearing just a towel. Her hair was still wet but she looked just as great as she had the previous night, maybe better. Henry had noticed a gradual change in Tammy over their brief time together. At first, she seemed to be playing the role of a hooker and although she had played the role very well, he sensed that wasn't her real self. He much preferred the woman who stood in front of him now.

"It's about time you woke up," Tammy said. "I thought I was going to have to hold a mirror to your face to find out if you were still breathing. You better get cracking. Check-out time is noon."

"Yeah, you're right," Henry said. "Give me a few minutes to take a shower. Interested in getting some breakfast?"

"Sure, although it's probably closer to lunch by now."

"Let's just call it brunch," Henry said as headed into the bathroom to take a shower. Henry took a quick shower and decided he also needed to shave as he was looking a bit scruffy. It seemed more important to him than usual that he try to look his best.

"I think the hotel has a pretty good restaurant," Henry shouted through the bathroom door, but didn't get a response. He figured she probably couldn't hear him over the noise of the ceiling fan in the bathroom which seemed to have a bit of squeak to it. He opened the door a crack. "I think the restaurant downstairs has a brunch buffet and my flight is not for a few more hours." Again, there was no response.

He opened the door fully, but Tammy was nowhere to be seen. He saw his pants lying on the floor with his wallet opened beside them. His heart stopped. How could he have been so stupid? He raced over and picked up his wallet, expecting to see his cash and credit cards gone. But the cash seemed to be all there, and all of his credit cards seemed to be there as well. The only thing missing were a few business cards that he kept in his wallet. He scanned the room looking for anything else missing. Then he saw one of his business cards propped up on a pillow. A small heart had been drawn on the front. He turned the business card over and read.

"Thank you. You were exactly what I needed."

*** CHAPTER 3 ***

Henry flew back to Toronto almost in a trance. He didn't remember checking out of the hotel or going through security at the airport, but he obviously had as the stewardess was now passing through the cabin advising the passengers to return their seats to the upright position as they would be landing in Toronto shortly.

Henry grabbed a cab and slumped into the back seat. He lived in a new neighbourhood west of Toronto located between Oakville and Burlington. He probably should have taken a shuttle as it would have been cheaper, but he had negotiated a flat fee with the cab driver rather than letting the meter run. This was against the rules but the cabbie had relented because he lived near Oakville himself and his work-day was almost over. He planned to head home after dropping off his last fare of the day.

As the cab approached his house, Henry could see his son David kicking a soccer ball from the green space alongside their property into a hockey net that was situated beside the garage to catch any errant shots. There weren't many errant shots. David was 17 years old and a very good soccer player. He played on his high school soccer team which was one of the top ranked teams in the province. Rumour was that he was on the radar of Canada's National Team, although no one would confirm or deny that speculation.

"Hi David," Henry yelled as he got out of the taxi and started to walk towards the house.

"Hi Dad," David said as he kicked the soccer ball which appeared to be headed directly towards Henry's head. Henry started to duck but the ball suddenly curved sharply and landed in the centre of the hockey net. David looked at him and grinned. Henry knew he had done it on purpose. That kid was getting a little too cocky for his own good.

Henry continued into the house and headed down the hallway towards his bedroom. He passed by his oldest son's bedroom on the way. "Hi Robert," he yelled, but only got a grunt as an acknowledgement. He was concentrating on some online video game. Robert was 19 years old and finished high school, but not really sure what he wanted to do with his life. He was good with computers and had worked as a day-trader over the summer and done quite well. For Robert, day-trading was almost like a video game as he bought and sold shares within seconds, making his money on the up or down ticks of the market.

Henry headed to the kitchen and grabbed himself a granola bar from the cupboard. He hadn't bothered to eat at the hotel. He looked out the kitchen window and could see Jenny working in the garden, so headed outside.

"Hi Sis," Henry said as he approached. "Thanks for watching the boys for me."

"No problem," Jenny said, looking over her shoulder at him. "You know those boys are old enough that they don't really need a sitter anymore."

"I know," Henry said, although he still didn't feel

comfortable leaving them alone since his wife had passed away over two years ago. They used to live in the heart of Toronto, but Henry found he couldn't continue to live in the same house after his wife had died. There were too many memories so he had used the life insurance money to purchase this new house. When he purchased it, it was out in the middle of nowhere although the neighbourhood had filled in quickly since then. His sons hadn't wanted to move, but they had adapted quickly and now seemed quite at home.

Jenny stood up from her gardening and looked at Henry. "Is everything OK?" she asked. "You look different somehow."

"Yeah, I'm fine. Where's Mom?" Henry asked, changing the subject.

"She went to the Seniors Centre." Henry's mother spent half of the year in Florida, but spent the rest of the year staying with either Henry or his sister.

"Oh, I almost forgot," Jenny said. "Alan called earlier in the week. He said he set aside a suit for you that he thinks you'll like."

Alan was Henry's younger brother. He worked at a store in downtown Toronto that specialized in men's suits and Alan seemed to call him about twice a year with an amazing deal on a new suit. However, Henry didn't wear suits as much as he used to so these great deals were just accumulating in the back of his closet. He wasn't even sure he had worn the last suit that he had purchased from Alan.

"I'll pop in to see him next week when I'm back in the office," Henry said. Henry walked back into the kitchen and caught David standing in front of the open fridge chugging down juice directly from the carton.

"How many times have I asked you to use a glass?" scolded Henry.

"It's OK, I'm planning to finish it," David said, which he did with one last gulp. "Hey Dad, we play for the high school regional championship up in Vaughan next Thursday afternoon. Do you think you'll be able to get off work to come watch us?"

"Probably, but I won't be able to say for sure until I see my schedule at the office next week. I'll do my best."

* * *

As Henry rode the train into Toronto on the following Monday morning, he found his thoughts wandering back to his night with Tammy. He could feel his heart beat faster and his body take on a warm glow. He thought about the note she had left on his business card, but had no idea what it meant.

"Mind if I sit here?" someone asked as they sat down without waiting for an answer. The train had stopped in Oakville to pick up more passengers. Henry nodded his acknowledgement to the business man who had just sat down, and proceeded to scan the faces of the other people on the train who had recently boarded. The train was now almost full, even though it was still rather early. Henry liked to catch an early train to avoid the crowds, but it seemed like the train was always busy these days, regardless of the time of day. Even though everyone was packed in beside each other, they all seemed to have an invisible wall between them. Some had their eyes closed listening to music or whatever was being piped into their ear-buds. Others were intently reading their newspapers, oblivious to the person doing the same thing standing mere inches away. It seemed every second person had their cell phone out with their thumbs gyrating back and forth as they sent text messages. And a few who were lucky enough to have found seats had their laptops open and getting an early start going through their emails.

Henry thought about the mountain of emails that were likely waiting for him when he arrived at the office. He had kept up with his email when they were working in Chicago last week, but he hadn't even thought about touching his laptop on Friday or over the weekend.

He stopped at the Tim Horton's located on the main floor of his office building and joined the long line of people who had the same addiction. The line, as always, moved quite quickly. Timmie's had mastered the process of getting people their morning fix with alarming efficiency.

"Medium double-double" said the girl behind the counter before Henry could even open his mouth. It amazed him how they remembered all of their regular customer's orders like they were stamped on their foreheads. Henry swiped his Timmie's card to pay for the coffee and headed up to his office on the 7th floor.

Henry spent all morning going through his email and updating his calendar. It was about 11:30 and his first scheduled meeting was at 1PM, so Henry decided he would take this opportunity to walk over to the menswear store where his brother worked. He wasn't sure when he would get another opportunity this week.

When Henry walked into the store, he saw Alan on one knee on the floor as he marked the hem on a customer's pair of pants. When that was completed, the customer returned to the change room and Alan turned his focus to another customer who was eyeing himself in a mirror sporting a new suit jacket he was considering.

"I think you'll have to go one size larger," Alan said, grabbing one quickly off of the rack.

"But I've always been a 42-regular," protested the customer.

"You haven't been a size 42 for ten years," countered

Alan, which was quickly confirmed when the customer tried on the larger size.

"Hi Alan," Henry said, trying to let Alan know he was there without interrupting his work with his current customers.

"Hey Bro," Alan said. "I'll be with you in two shakes."

Alan was working with several customers at once whereas there were other clerks at the store who seemed to be doing busy work or waiting for customers to show up. Alan quickly grabbed a shirt and tie from the hundreds that were scattered on various displays in the store and quickly slid them into the suit jacket that was sitting on the check-out counter, just as the customer that had been trying on the pants emerged from the change-room.

"I think this shirt and tie would go nicely with that suit," Alan said as the customer approached.

"They do look quite nice," said the customer, "although I can't see myself wearing a purple shirt. I usually just wear a white shirt with my suits."

"It's time to move out of the middle-ages," countered Alan, holding up the suit jacket, shirt and tie so the customer could see. Even Henry could see that this combination worked and instantly made the customer look ten years younger.

"Sold," said the customer, and Alan quickly rang up the sale.

Alan turned his focus to his brother. "I've got a great suit for you, but I need a smoke-break. Do you have time?"

"Sure," Henry said as he followed Alan out through the back room and through a door that led out to an alley behind the store. Alan grabbed a piece of wood that was lying on the floor and stuck it in the door so it didn't lock behind them. Henry noticed that the piece of wood had a large "G" carved into it, which struck him as odd since the name of the store began with a "B".

"What does the G stand for?" Henry asked.

"Nothing," Alan replied. "I just carve initials into stuff while I'm out here on my smoke breaks." Henry noticed several other G's carved into the bricks on the back of the building. There were several other graffiti marks scattered on the wall so it was obviously a hobby of other people as well.

"I just made more money on that shirt and tie than I did on the suit," Alan said, changing the subject as he lit up a cigarette.

Alan was about six years younger than Henry. You could easily tell they were brothers, even though Alan weighed at least 40 pounds less. He had always been a little hyper-active which somewhat explained why he was so thin, but the cigarette smoking was also a factor. Henry could see from the mound of cigarette butts that lay on the ground that Alan was still a heavy smoker. Henry also knew that Alan smoked things other than regular cigarettes on a regular basis as well.

"We've been really busy," Alan said. "We had a big 48-hour sale on the weekend and sold a ton of stuff. They ran an ad in this morning's paper saying that due to the overwhelming response, they had extended the sale until 5PM today, so we've been getting more people in today. Of course, we knew all along the sale would include today to catch the people who don't want to come downtown on the weekends."

"Whatever works," Henry said. Henry knew that Alan was a great salesman, but he also knew he worked incredibly hard.

"I only have a few minutes to measure you up for the suit I put aside for you," Alan said. "I've got Edward Bronson coming in for a custom fitting at 1PM." Edward

Bronson was a big player in Toronto. His family owned one of Toronto's biggest newspapers and several others across the country. They also had part ownership in some TV stations in Toronto, Calgary and Vancouver. Henry knew that Alan was trying to impress him, and it was working.

"No problem," Henry said. "I've got a one o'clock meeting myself. I'm surprised Edward Bronson buys suits at a discount menswear store."

"He doesn't buy stuff off of our regular rack. We bring in higher quality stuff for some of our special clients. We've got a few of them - a few bank presidents, a bunch of lawyers. Do you know Frenchie Bouchard? He wears our stuff on the air all the time. We give him a good deal because we get mentioned in the credits."

Of course Henry knew who Frenchie Bouchard was. François Bouchard was a sportscaster on one of the national sports channels and one of their most popular personalities. He was a promising hockey player with the Montreal Canadiens until he blew out his knee. He had originally just appeared on one of the French channels as a colour commentator while he went through numerous knee operations, but when the doctors finally determined that his hockey career was over, he quickly decided that being a sports commentator would be his new career. It was major news when it was announced that he was leaving the local Montreal station and moving to a national sports channel.

The percentage of female viewers of the sports channel had grown dramatically since his arrival at the network. It was funny that hockey players and male viewers always referred to him as Frenchie, which was how he was known in his playing days. However, the female viewers referred to him as François, and there was normally a bit of a swoon when they said his name. He would certainly be a good promoter for the store. He seemed to be wearing a new suit or sports jacket on the air every couple of weeks. He wore everything from flashy gold sports jackets to classic looking pinstripe suits, and everything in between, and looked good in all of them.

Alan took one last puff on his cigarette, threw it on the ground with all of the others, and then stepped on it to make sure it was out. He lifted up the stick that was holding the door ajar and they stepped back into the backroom of the store. Alan went to a rack that contained all of the clothes that were waiting for tailoring or pickup and selected the suit that he had set aside for Henry. Henry noticed that it had a price tag of $1,200.

"I can't afford to pay $1,200 for a suit," Henry said, looking a little worried.

"Don't worry," Alan said. "You won't be paying anywhere close to that."

Alan carried the suit out into the main part of the store and slipped the jacket onto Henry. It fit perfectly. Alan pulled the pants from the hanger, handed them to Henry and directed him to the change room to try them on. When Henry emerged from the change room, Alan asked him to stand in front of the mirror so he could mark them up for alterations.

"It looks like you've put on a few pounds," Alan said as he marked on the pants where the waist would have to be let out. He then dropped to the floor where he marked where they would have to be hemmed. "They should be ready by Thursday."

"That reminds me," Henry said, "David has a soccer game up in Vaughan on Thursday - regional finals. Any chance you can make it?"

"Maybe," Alan said. "I'm off on Thursdays, so probably. I'll let you know."

Henry returned to the change room to take off the pants. When he emerged, Alan wasn't there. He saw him over in another part of the store that had been cordoned off and saw Edward Bronson talking to Alan as he tried on a suit jacket. Mr. Bronson had arrived early, or more precisely, his entourage had arrived early. The owner of the store was there as well, trying to make sure everything ran smoothly. Alan looked over and caught Henry's eye, and then nodded for him to place the pants he had just tried on onto the counter. Henry nodded back, placed them on the counter and started to head back to his office.

*** CHAPTER 4 ***

On Thursday morning Henry rode the train into Toronto as usual. He had arranged to catch a ride with Alan out to the soccer game later in the afternoon. David would be going to the game on a school bus with the rest of the team. The only problem was Henry's mom. She was always keen to attend her grandson's soccer games and since this was the regional finals, she wasn't going to miss this game for the world. She had her own car, but she didn't like driving on the 400-series highways and Henry wasn't keen on her driving on the expressways either. Henry had encouraged Robert to come cheer on his brother, partly because he knew Robert would drive rather than his mom.

Henry worked through lunch to make sure his schedule was cleared for later in the day. He knew that problems had a habit of showing up at the worst possible time. His phone rang just as he was packing up and getting ready to leave, but he decided to ignore it and let it go to voice-mail.

Since Alan didn't work on Thursdays and didn't want to drive downtown, they had arranged that Henry would take the subway out to the Kennedy station and Alan would pick him up at the station. It was close to Alan's apartment and would probably save them at least 45 minutes in getting out of the downtown. When Henry emerged from the station, he spotted Alan double-parked in a no stopping zone. He quickly jumped into the passenger seat and threw his stuff onto the back seat.

"What's with the bling?" Henry asked, noticing that Alan was wearing a leather jacket and a rather large gold chain around his neck. "Are you supposed to be Starsky or Hutch?" Henry asked, referring to the 1970's cop show.

"I have to bring enough style for the both of us," smirked Alan.

Alan sped out of the subway station's parking lot and started the drive to Vaughan, which is just north of Toronto. Alan always drove fast, but he seemed to be driving even faster than normal today.

"We've got lots of time to make it to the game," Henry said, glancing at his watch and hoping that his comment would cause Alan to slow down a bit. It didn't.

When they got to the soccer field, Henry was pleased to see his mother already sitting in the stands with Robert sitting beside her. Henry climbed up the steps taking two at a time and sat down beside Robert. Alan followed and sat down beside his mom. Since Alan wasn't married and didn't have any kids, his mom didn't spend as much time visiting him as she did with Henry or Jenny.

"Thanks for driving Grandma to the game," Alan whispered to Robert. He knew that was the main reason that Robert had come. Robert could always be counted on to come through when needed.

They turned their focus to the field where David's team, the Warriors, were going through their warm-ups. This consisted of a series of stretches, runs and jumps which the team did in unison.

"Doesn't David look like Alan when he was younger?" Grandma asked. Alan said he couldn't see it, but Henry knew exactly what she was talking about. He had noticed it for the last few years.

"How could you not see it?" Henry said. "He's the spitting image of you when you were seventeen. He not only looks like you, but he walks and runs exactly like you. Hell, he even sounds like you."

"I think he's much more athletic than I ever was," Alan said.

Alan had been a very good athlete in high school and naturally good in all sports, although he hadn't worked at it at all. He could have made any sports team he wanted and had been asked to try out for several high school teams by the coaches, but had never shown much interest and spent most of his high school years skipping class and hanging out in the pool hall.

David was totally different from Alan in that aspect. David worked hard at everything he did, including sports. That's probably why David was being watched by the scouts. Having raw talent was essential, but having desire and a strong work ethic were equally important.

The referee blew his whistle indicating that the warm-up period was over and he summoned the team captains to centre-field for the coin flip. This would be a tough game for David's team, partly because they were using their backup goalkeeper due to an injury, but also because they were facing the top-ranked team from Vaughan and the stands were now filled with their supporters. The regional finals were always held in Vaughan because they had the best facilities. This year the Vaughan team had won their division so, in effect, they had home field advantage.

David had said they'd be playing a much more defensive strategy this game due to their injured keeper and the team had been working on defense all week at their practices. David's position with the Warriors was right defense and he knew he would be under pressure the whole game because their opponent's best striker played on his side. To their surprise, their opponent also seemed to be playing a very defensive formation. The first half ended with no score, and really no good scoring chances for either team. The people in the stands were getting increasingly bored with the lack of offense and the Vaughan supporters had tried to fire their team up with numerous cheers. The players on the field seemed oblivious to anything going on in the stands, but it certainly fired up Alan. He had tried to organize cheers for David's team without success and now seemed to be getting into verbal assaults with the Vaughan supporters. Henry switched seats to sit beside Alan so he could try to calm him down.

"Take it easy," he said to Alan, encouraging him to sit down. "We don't want to be starting any fights in the stands. In case you haven't noticed, we're severely out-numbered." Alan said he was going for a smoke and started heading out of the stands. Henry went with him to make sure he didn't get into any trouble along the way.

"I don't think they allow smoking anywhere close to the stands," Henry said when they reached the bottom of the stands. "We better head over to the far side of the parking lot." Henry had no idea if that was true or not, but he wanted to get Alan as far away from the Vaughan supporters as he could.

"Have you been taking your meds?" Henry asked. Alan had been diagnosed as being bipolar a few years ago and had gone through some rough patches, although he had been doing much better over the last year.

"Yeah, I took them this morning," Alan said. "I've been taking them every second day because I'm almost out and I haven't had time to get to the drugstore to get my prescription filled. I went today but they told me to come back later today to pick them up."

"Make sure you do," Henry said. "You seem a little wired today."

"I'm fine. I'm just excited about the game." Alan took one last drag on his cigarette and they headed back to the stands just as the second half of the game was getting underway.

The second half of the game followed the same pattern as the first half. The Vaughan team was using a trap strategy where they would quickly converge on a player whenever the Warriors moved the ball up to midfield. The midfielder had nowhere to go with the ball and the only safe pass was back to the defender. This is what the Warriors had done in the first half of the game, but they were growing impatient with their lack of offence. The few times they had tried to force a pass through the middle had resulted in turnovers and the Vaughan team had quickly mounted a counter-attack that had resulted in three good scoring chances. Once they had hit the cross-bar, once their rookie goalkeeper had made a great save, and once David had cleared the ball just before the ball crossed the line. They were lucky the game was still scoreless. Their coach had reminded them to stay with their defensive strategy at half-time, but it was easier said than done, and the players could sense the uneasiness growing in Marc, their goalkeeper.

"Come on guys, we need a goal," Marc said. "Move the ball. You've got to move the ball quicker. Somebody's got to make a play." Marc was a great goalkeeper, although he was only in grade nine and wasn't used to the pressure. He had been quite happy being the backup and sitting on the bench all season long, but had suddenly been thrust into the spotlight with the injury to their regular keeper. David and the other defenders had continually been encouraging him throughout the game, but they could see that he was now having trouble making even routine saves from long range shots. During a stoppage in play due to an injury, several of the Warriors gathered together along the sidelines to get a drink of water.

"We've got to get the ball out of our end," David said. "Marc's getting more and more nervous and we've got to give him a break so he can calm down."

"That's why Michael went down," James said. "I don't think he's really hurt." James was one of the Warriors best strikers but had hardly touched the ball because he had been marked closely for the whole game. "It seems like they've got all of their best players up front or at midfield. Alex, you've probably got the strongest leg. Just hit me a long ball and I'll try to run under it and put some pressure on their defence for a while."

Alex played middle defence and knew he could easily do it, but seemed reluctant. "Coach said he wants us to just do short passes and play a defensive strategy."

David put his hand on Alex's shoulder. "I know," David said. "If it doesn't work out, I'll take the heat from the coach but we've got to try something different. I don't like our chances if it goes to a shoot-out."

And that's exactly where it looked like it was heading as regulation time had now elapsed and they were now into injury time, which they expected would only be three or four minutes. The Warriors tried one last push up the left side of the field, but once again their opponents converged on the ball using their trapping strategy. The midfielder realized all of his passing lanes were cut off and his only option was to pass the ball back to the left defender who did a short pass over to Alex at middle defence. Alex looked down the field for James but could see he was being held by one of the Vaughan defenders and couldn't get away.

David had noticed throughout the game that the Vaughan team had gradually shifted farther and farther to the left side of the field as the game went on, which made sense because the Warriors had tried to go up the left side about eighty percent of the time. David was pretty much all by himself on the right side. He was supposed to fall back behind Alex in this situation as part of their defensive strategy, but instead suddenly took off down the field and called for the ball.

"David, where the hell are you going?" yelled the coach. "Get back!!!"

David didn't hear him, or pretended not to hear him, and kept racing down the right side of the field. Alex launched a long arcing pass towards David. The Vaughan midfielder was scrambling to get back into position and looked like he would intercept the pass, but David leapt high in the air, flicked the ball over the charging midfielder, and raced by him to gain control of the ball. The whole right side of the field had opened up like the parting of the Red Sea and David only had one defender to beat. David gave him his best move, but to no avail. The defender was successfully angling David further to the right and away from the goal.

"David," shouted James, calling for the ball. James was at the left side of the box, uncovered. David crossed the ball towards him, trying to make sure it was high enough to clear the goalkeeper who stood between them. Both James and the goalkeeper jumped as high as they could trying to reach the ball, but it was too high for both of them.

"Damn," David said as the ball bounced away.

"David, get back," his coach continued to yell. Even

Henry was shouting for his son to get back, fearful of Vaughan's powerful counter-attack. But David continued in toward the Vaughan net. Their keeper had fallen to the ground in a heap in his attempt to reach the ball and was now scrambling to get back into position. James had managed to keep his feet and was now racing after the ball, which he reached before it went out of bounds. There must have been five Vaughan players converging on James. James blindly launched the ball back towards the net.

David was standing alone in front of the open net, with no defender to be seen. The goalkeeper had fallen again and was now half-crawling to get back into position. You could almost see the smile get larger and larger on David's face as the ball arced towards him and he knew he was going to score. It seemed like everything was in slow motion and it felt like it took half an hour for the ball to reach him. But when it did, he calmly headed the ball into the back of the net.

The Warrior supporters in the stands let out an enormous cheer. The Vaughan supporters were screaming that the play was offside. The referee ran towards the net and checked with his assistant on the sidelines who still had his flag down. The referee blew his whistle and pointed at centre-field indicating it was a good goal.

The Warriors were all jumping up and down and hugging each other. Most of the Vaughan players had slumped to the ground knowing they had lost, but a few were still complaining to the referee. When they started play again, it was only a few seconds until the referee blew his whistle twice indicating the game was over.

Alan was jumping up and down in the stands pumping his fist in the air, and continuing to taunt some of the Vaughan supporters. "We're number one! We're number one! We're number one!"

"Sit down and shut up," yelled one of the Vaughan supporters, "or I'll come down there and shut your mouth for you!"

Alan started up the stands toward the man but Henry quickly grabbed him and pulled him back. "Come on, Alan. Just let it go. Let's go congratulate David."

Some of the parents and fans had congregated along the fence behind the team bench offering their congratulations. When Alan saw this, he raced down the stairs to join the celebration. Henry could see David who was being congratulated by two girls. He recognized Ashley because she was on the girl's high school team. Henry was pretty sure that Ashley was interested in David because she seemed to hang around after the girls soccer practices finished to talk to David as the boys soccer practice was getting ready to start.

When Alan reached David, he almost pushed the girls aside when he gave David a high-five. "Time to intervene," thought Henry as he hurried down the stairs. If it was a choice between being congratulated by an uncle or two girls, Henry was pretty sure which option David preferred.

"Alan, I have to grab my stuff out of the back of your car," Henry said when he got there, steering Alan away.

"Congratulations son," Henry said as they walked away, "although you may have been a little out of position on that play."

"Yeah," David shouted back. "Coach said he wants to discuss that with me at the next practice."

"See you at home," Henry yelled, giving David a thumbs-up sign.

Henry and Alan continued to talk about the goal as they headed back towards the car. Alan seemed more excited about the win than any of the players and Henry struggled to keep him under control.

"It's David's birthday on Sunday," Henry said. "It would be great if you could come out to our place on Sunday afternoon. Just family. David's going out later with his friends to celebrate, but will tolerate cake with his family as a pre-party."

"Any idea what he'd like for a present?" Alan asked.

"He said he wants an official soccer ball from the last world cup," Henry answered. "I was going to buy him one a few months ago when the World Cup was going on but they were priced out of the world. I think the price will have dropped by now, but I can't find them in any of the stores. If you can track one down, I'm sure he'd love it. I'm not sure why he wants another soccer ball, but he's been trying to collect the official World Cup balls. No imitations."

"I'll see if I can track one down," Alan said. "I'll see you on Sunday."

*** CHAPTER 5 ***

On Sunday afternoon, the family gathered to celebrate David's 18th birthday. David was smiling and thanking everyone for the cake and the presents they had got him, but Henry noticed David checking his watch several times during the festivities. He sensed that David was more interested in the party his friends were planning for him later that night.

Alan had not shown for the party, but had couriered a present for David, along with a note expressing his apologies for missing the party. Henry knew what was in the package as he watched David open it, but he was surprised when he detected a bit of disappointment on David's face.

There was a knock on the door and Henry could see Alex standing on the front porch through the window. Alex was more than a teammate to David – he was his best friend. Alex had organized the birthday party for David and had come to pick him up.

"Gotta go," David said. "Thanks everybody for the cake and presents."

Henry followed David to the door. "Don't let things get too wild tonight and make sure you behave yourself," Henry said. "Will there be any alcohol at this party tonight?"

"We won't be doing any drinking," Alex answered. "Coach would kill us. We've got the provincial championship coming up." Henry wasn't naïve enough to think there wouldn't be any liquor at all, but he also knew David and Alex were both good kids and very responsible.

Henry pulled David back around the corner of the entranceway where Alex couldn't hear them. "You looked a little disappointed with the World Cup soccer ball that Uncle Alan sent you," Henry said. "I told him that's what you wanted, so don't blame him if I steered him wrong."

David paused, not sure if he should say anything or not. "It's fine. But it's not the official one." He picked up the ball which was still in the box and spun the ball to reveal a "Goliath" logo where the "Adidas" logo should have been. Other than that, it looked like a high-quality soccer ball. Since Henry was a golfer, he knew of a company called Goliath that made golf clubs. It was pretty good stuff, but without the higher prices found in the name companies like TaylorMade, Titleist and Nike. Maybe they also made equipment for other sports as well.

"Alan probably didn't know," Henry said. "Keep the ball and I'll try to find an official Adidas ball for you."

"Thanks Dad," David said as he headed out the door. "Don't wait up."

Henry always found it hard to go to sleep when he knew one of his kids was still out. Sure enough, he was lying awake in bed when he heard David come into the house just passed midnight. It was only then that he fell asleep. The alarm seemed to sound only a few seconds later, but a quick check of the clock indicated it was 6:30AM. Henry wiped the sleep out of his eyes and headed for the shower. He was heading off to Chicago today for another meeting with the firm they were merging with. It was just a one-day trip and he would be flying back to Toronto tonight. His thoughts turned to Tammy, but were quickly interrupted by the ringing of his cell phone. It was Alan.

"Hey Bro," Alan said. "Hope I didn't wake you. Sorry I couldn't make David's party yesterday but I thought I'd let you know that your suit is ready. I've got two tickets to the junior all-star hockey game tonight so I could just bring the suit with me if you want to go to the game."

"I don't think I'll be able to go," Henry said. "I'm going to Chicago for the day and my flight doesn't get back until 7:45PM."

"That doesn't matter," Alan said. "I'll probably be late myself. It's just an exhibition game so doesn't matter if we're late. How about I meet you by the Will-Call ticket booth about 8:45PM?"

"I'll try," Henry replied, "but don't count on it. I'll call you on your cell if my flight is delayed."

Henry's meeting in Chicago that day ended earlier than expected. He had arrived at the airport for the flight back to Toronto much earlier than he needed to, even for an international flight. He knew it was foolish but he still scanned the crowd of people at the airport hoping to see Tammy. He had even gone to the same restaurant and the same bar as before hoping he would see her, but no such luck.

Henry's flight was pretty much on time and he caught a cab to the arena to meet his brother. Sure enough, Alan was waiting by the ticket booths holding at least three suit bags over his shoulder.

"I hope those aren't all for me," Henry said as he approached.

"No. Only one. The other two are sports jackets for Frenchie Bouchard. He's doing the game tonight and the hockey tickets are compliments of him."

They walked into the arena and headed towards the press boxes and broadcast booths on one of the upper levels. The first period had just ended and they could see Frenchie and the play-by-play man discussing the first period highlights on the air. Henry was surprised to see how tiny their broadcast booth was. They were standing in front of a bright green screen with the camera only a few feet in front of them. When he looked at the TV monitor to the side, he could see a play from the first period being displayed to their left with Frenchie pointing out the positioning of the players as the play developed. When he looked back at the broadcast booth, Frenchie seemed to be gesturing in mid-air. That was the magic of television.

"Frenchie asked me to bring him a couple of sports jackets for the next few broadcasts," Alan said. An under-19 all-star team from Sweden had come to Canada to play some exhibition games against a Canadian all-star team made up from players from the OHL. "After tonight, they head to Stockholm to play some games over there and Frenchie will be covering the games."

The bright lights and the green screen suddenly went dark. They were now in a commercial break and people were quickly re-positioning to get ready for the second period. Suit jackets were removed and ties loosened because they would not be on-camera as they broadcast the play-by-play in the next period. Frenchie saw Alan standing in the wings and came over to him. "Thanks for bringing these over," Frenchie said as he approached.

"Make sure you get them pressed before you go on the air over there," Alan said. "They'll probably get wrinkled in the baggage and we want you looking your best."

Alan introduced Henry to Frenchie. Frenchie shook his hand and said how good it was to meet him, but Henry could tell that his focus had already shifted to getting ready for the broadcast of the second period. Henry and Alan headed to their assigned seats for the game, which were near centre-ice about ten rows behind the Canadian bench.

"It must be nice to know people in high places," Henry said as he sat down.

"You have no idea," Alan replied.

* * *

The next day Frenchie was half asleep as he headed off of the plane in Stockholm. He'd never been able to sleep on airplanes and this was no exception. He'd come to Sweden with Darren, his regular play-by-play announcer, a producer, a production assistant and a technician. They'd be using a local camera crew and using the main feed for the game from the local Swedish broadcaster.

The others had managed to get some sleep on the flight, so they were much more chipper than Frenchie. Since they were trying to keep costs under control, Frenchie and Darren were sharing a room at the hotel. When the bell-hop brought their bags to their room, Frenchie told him to wait as he wanted to send his suit jackets out to be pressed.

"I'm not sure they need it," Darren said, holding up one of the suit jackets. "It looks like they didn't get wrinkled at all during the flight."

"I still want to get them pressed," Frenchie said as he took them from Darren and handed them to the bell-hop. "Make sure they're pressed by Elsa" Frenchie said to the bell-hop. "I was told to ask for her specifically as she was highly recommended."

"Yes sir," replied the bell-hop. "I'll make sure she handles it personally." Frenchie slipped the bell-hop a generous tip as he thanked him.

When the bell-hop brought Frenchie's sports jackets to the laundry in the basement of the hotel, he placed them on the counter and waved to Elsa who was in the middle of pressing someone's tuxedo. "Some hot shot said he wants you to personally press his sports jackets," he shouted. "I think they look fine as they are."

"It's OK," Elsa said. "I'll take care of it."

She immediately came over to get the sports jackets and took them into the back room. She felt along the hem of the first sports jacket, but didn't feel a thing. She repeated the procedure with the second sports jacket and her eyes lit up when she felt what she was looking for. She grabbed a seam ripper from the various tools on the bench and carefully opened the seam. She pulled a small plastic object from inside the seam and placed it inside the pocket of her smock.

"I have to head out to run some errands," Elsa said to her co-workers. "I should be back in about half an hour." Elsa headed out of the hotel and walked about six blocks until she came to a medium-sized building with three initials and a strange logo on it.

"I'd like to see Anders," she said when she got to the reception area.

"Do you have an appointment?" asked the receptionist.

"No, just tell him I have a message from Goliath. I'm sure he'll see me." The receptionist looked confused, but called Anders on her phone. He arrived almost immediately and took Elsa back to his office.

"I believe this is for you," Elsa said as she gave him the small plastic object.

Anders examined it briefly and then reached into his own pocket and pulled out a similar looking object. "And I believe this is for you."

Elsa took the object and placed it in her pocket. Anders escorted her back out to the reception area and Elsa began her walk back to the hotel. When she got back to the hotel, she placed the new object back into the hem of Frenchie's sports jacket and quickly sewed it up again. She gave both sports jackets a quick press and placed them inside some plastic bags.

"These can be returned to the guest," Elsa said to the bell-hop.

*** CHAPTER 6 ***

On Thursday morning Henry was up earlier than normal as he was heading off to Chicago yet again. The merger had now been approved by the partners and activities would now be shifting from the planning and budgeting stages to the implementation stage. Henry expected he would be spending two to three days a week in Chicago over the next month as they converted their legal accounting system and some other software so the entire firm would be on the same platform.

As Henry headed into the kitchen, he was surprised to see David sitting at the kitchen table gulping down some cereal. "What are you doing up so early?" Henry asked.

"Coach wants us in before class today to continue working on conditioning," David replied. The provincial championships were being held in Barrie this year and less than two weeks away. "Hey Dad, they told us last week that all of the teams will be staying at the Sunset Resort for the weekend of the tournament."

The Sunset Resort was located on one of the lakes just north of Barrie. During the summer months, they catered to families as it offered boating, swimming, beach volleyball, mini-putt golfing and numerous other activities. The parents could sign their kids up for a variety of supervised activities depending on their age and interests, yet get to spend time with them at the scheduled mealtimes or in their cabins in the evening. It wasn't anything fancy as the owners tried to retain a bit of a rustic feel at the resort. David was familiar with the resort because he had worked there the previous summer helping as an activities coordinator and at the front desk.

Now that the summer was over, the resort catered to specialized groups and corporate retreats. This was a good place to house all of the teams coming for the provincial championships because they could keep all of the teams together and it would be much cheaper than putting them up in hotels and feeding them in restaurants.

"They had actually called me to ask if I could work that weekend, but I told them I couldn't because I was on one of the teams," David said.

Henry checked his watch and realized he'd have to hurry to catch his flight. "Gotta run, but my trip to Chicago is just a day-trip so you can fill me in on the rest of the details later tonight." He grabbed a couple of granola bars from the pantry and headed off to the airport.

Henry spent most of the morning working with the accounting staff on the timing and the details of converting their system to the same legal accounting system used by RBT. A couple of the staff were quite keen on the conversion as their system was old and dated and they looked forward to using more modern software, but the head of the accounting department was somewhat reluctant as she had been using the existing system since she started with the firm over fifteen years ago.

They broke for lunch about 11:30 which suited Henry

just fine because the granola bars he'd scarfed down on the way to the airport were not going to hold him very much longer. Henry left the building in search of a place to grab a quick lunch. He was standing on the corner of Michigan and Grand waiting for a traffic light when he saw her. Not Tammy, but Samantha. At least he was pretty sure it was her.

The "Walk" sign lit up and the throngs of people started across Michigan Avenue. Henry stayed where he was as Samantha was crossing the street toward him. When he called her name, she looked up and he could see the confusion in her face as she scanned the faces of the dozens of people walking towards her looking for whoever had called her name. Henry called her name again and she quickly locked in on him. She smiled at him but Henry could tell she didn't really recognize him. He could almost see the wheels spinning in her head as she tried to place where she'd seen him before. He noticed the change in her expression when she remembered.

"Hi Samantha," he said as she reached his side of the street. "I'm Henry Shaw. I need to see Tammy."

"That's not her real name you know," she replied as she continued walking.

Henry turned and started to walk beside her. "I know, that's the name of her cat, but I really need to see her again. She never told me her real name."

"Look, you were exactly what she needed at the time, but I'm not sure she wants to see you again," Samantha said, continuing to walk.

Henry grabbed her arm, forcing her to stop. "Yeah, she wrote that on the card, but I have no idea what that means. I think she owes me more than that."

Samantha was familiar with the whole story because Tammy had spoken about it for hours and hours the next day. She knew that it was just supposed to be a one night stand, but she knew it had been more than that for Tammy and she was now sensing that it had been more than that for Henry as well. She felt sorry for him, but she had also been sworn to secrecy by her best friend. "I'll tell her that you want to see her again," she said, "but that's all I can do. It's up to her to decide what she wants to do. I'm sorry."

Henry could see in her eyes that she truly was sorry. "How can I reach you?" Henry asked as Samantha started to walk away.

"You can't," Samantha replied, looking back over her shoulder. "If she wants to see you again, we'll find you. Remember, we have your card." She smiled at him, but Henry could sense it was almost a smile of pity. He watched her walk away and into the Chicago Tribune tower.

Henry thought about Tammy throughout his flight back to Toronto later that day. After his flight landed, he headed to the parkade to get his car and as he drove through the bumper to bumper traffic on his way home, he thought about what he could have said differently to Samantha to convince her to let him see Tammy again, but he was at a loss.

As he pulled into his driveway, he had an immediate sense that something was wrong. David was kicking the soccer ball alongside the garage as usual, but he headed directly toward his dad as soon as he saw the car.

"What's wrong?" Henry asked as he opened his car door.

"It's Uncle Alan," David said. "He's acting all crazy. He was here when I got home from school. He seems really spaced out. Robert's inside keeping an eye on him but I couldn't stay in there with him. I'm sorry Dad, but he was freaking me out."

Henry headed into the kitchen of the house and could see his brother pacing in the living room and waving his arms wildly as he was recounting some story to his mother. Alan was wearing his leather coat with numerous gold chains around his neck. He was also wearing a hat that seemed much too small perched on the side of his head, along with sunglasses that had a blue tint to them. He looked just like a pimp that Henry had recently seen in an old movie on TV.

Robert had seen Henry come through the back door into the kitchen and quietly slipped out of the living room to talk to his dad. Alan seemed oblivious to his surroundings as he continued to talk about some fantastic adventure he'd had.

"What's going on?" Henry whispered to Robert as he came into the kitchen.

"I don't really know," Robert replied. "He showed up this afternoon looking for you, but he's been talking to Grandma non-stop for the last two hours. It's almost like he's on drugs or something. He's completely wired. I've been keeping an eye on him, but he doesn't seem violent or anything, just hyper."

"How did he get here?" Henry asked. "I didn't see his car in the driveway."

"He came in a limousine," Robert said. "It was like he was some kind of a rock star. The neighbours were all gawking wondering who he was. He's carrying a wad of cash and said he gave the driver a $500 tip for his troubles."

"Thanks for keeping an eye on him," Henry said. "I'm going to go talk to him. When I do, can you try to get Grandma out of there?" Robert nodded his agreement.

"Hi Alan," Henry said loudly as he entered the living room. "What brings you out here?"

Alan stopped telling whatever story he was in the middle of recounting and seemed to be jolted back into realizing where he was. Robert signaled to his grandma to come into the kitchen. She hesitated, a little apprehensive about leaving Alan in his current state, but moved into the kitchen when she saw Henry gesture with his eyes.

"Hey Bro," Alan said, moving towards him and giving him a hug as if he hadn't seen him in twenty years.

Henry hugged him back just as hard, and then looked him straight in the eye. "Have you been taking your medications?"

"I lost them," Alan replied, looking somewhat embarrassed. "I just got a new prescription filled and had them in a bag in my car, but I can't seem to find them."

"Where's your car?"

"I don't know. That's the problem. If I could find my fucking car, I could find my pills."

"When's the last time you slept?"

"I'm not sure. Probably a couple of days ago, but I'm not tired. When I try to sleep, my mind just races." Alan slumped to the couch, having suddenly realized how tired he was.

Henry had seen Alan in this state before, although it had been a few years. Alan's bipolar condition was normally kept under control provided he stayed on his medications. However, when he stopped taking them, he would fluctuate wildly between being in a manic state where he couldn't sleep at all to sleeping for days at a time. The extravagant jewelry, clothes and rock star persona were clear indications that Alan was in one of his manic states. There was no way of knowing what he could have said or done over the last few days. Henry looked with concern at Alan as he slumped back on the couch. He was out like a light within seconds, which was probably a good thing.

Henry walked back into the kitchen. "Are you OK?" Henry asked his mother.

"Yes, I'm fine," she replied. "What about Alan? He's been telling me he's been travelling around the world. He said he's supposed to meet the President in Washington next week and then travel to Europe the following week."

"Don't believe anything he's saying," Henry said.

"Why would he lie?" she asked. "It doesn't seem like he's lying. He's been telling me about all of the famous people he's been meeting."

"He doesn't think he is lying," Henry said. "He's hallucinating, so it seems like it's actually happened to him. Remember we went through something like this with him a few years ago." She did remember, but she never really understood it.

They had supper as Alan continued to sleep on the couch. Henry said he would take his brother to see his doctor the next morning so he could get him back on the proper medications.

Later that night, Henry could tell that David was still spooked by the day's events. He stopped by his bedroom just before bedtime.

"Are you OK?" Henry asked.

"Yeah, I'm fine," David replied, but Henry could tell that he wasn't.

"Dad…" he started to say. "Do you think I'll end up being crazy like Uncle Alan when I get older?"

"He's not crazy," Henry said. Henry explained what a bipolar condition was, trying to remember how the doctors had explained it to him a few years ago. "Why do you think you'll end up like Uncle Alan?"

"Well, everyone says I'm just like Uncle Alan. I look like him and act like him when he was my age. I just wondered if I'm going to end up in the same condition as he is when I'm older."

"No, you're not the same person as he is," Henry said. "Of course we always inherit some things from our families. My dad had high blood pressure so I have a higher chance of having it. In fact, I do, but I can control it with my high blood pressure medication. It's the same thing with other conditions like arthritis, high cholesterol or in this situation, being bipolar. And Alan did some things when he was younger that probably made his condition worse."

"What do you mean?" David asked.

"Well, don't tell Grandma," Henry said, "but Alan smoked a lot of pot when he was younger, and I think he still does."

"So his condition was caused by him smoking pot?" David asked.

"No, I didn't say that. Anyone can be diagnosed as being bipolar. Smoking pot didn't cause it, but I read an article in a magazine a few months ago that said it seems that people who smoke a lot of pot experience worse symptoms than people who don't. I think they're continuing to research what really causes it." Henry sensed that he had somewhat relieved David's anxiety, but not completely. "Good night," Henry said as he pulled David's bedroom door closed.

"Good night Dad." As Henry walked away from David's bedroom, he heard the click as David locked his bedroom door. David was obviously still a little spooked by having Alan in the house.

Henry headed back into the living room to check on Alan, but he was still out cold. Henry knew that tomorrow would be a long day so he decided to head to bed himself, but he kept his bedroom door open so he'd hear Alan if or when he woke up. Henry fell asleep as soon as his head hit the pillow, but was jolted awake when he heard Alan arguing with someone in the living room. He glanced at the clock-radio beside his bed and saw that it was 3:15AM. He quickly got out of bed and headed out into the living room to see Alan was by himself, but he was yelling into his cell phone. The other voices that Alan had heard were actually coming from the TV which had the volume set nearly to the max. Henry grabbed the remote and turned the volume down.

"Alan, you've got to keep it down. People are trying to sleep." When Alan saw Henry, he quickly ended his telephone call.

"Who are you arguing with at this time of night?" Henry asked.

"It's not the middle of the night where they are," Alan replied, seeming reluctant to let Henry know who he was talking to. "It wasn't important."

"It sure sounded important by the way you were yelling at whoever that was." Alan looked like he was going to respond, but then seemed to stop himself.

"So what's going on?" Henry asked. "Mom said you were telling her weird stories about spies, world travel and meeting famous people."

Alan seemed confused and a little alarmed. "She's crazy," Alan said.

"Right back at you," Henry said. "I figured it was caused by you being off your meds. So, who were you yelling at over the phone?"

Alan looked a little sheepish. "It's someone from overseas. We've been working on something together." Alan then launched into some fantastic story about people he was working with in Sweden, Greece, South Africa and numerous other countries. Henry could see Alan getting more and more worked up as he told his stories. Henry could hardly follow them as he flipped from one story to the next. Alan seemed to be getting louder and louder as he worked himself into a frenzy. Henry hugged him and tried to get Alan to calm down. It seemed to work as Alan slumped onto the couch again. Alan pulled Henry towards him and whispered into his ear, as if he was going to tell him his deepest, darkest secret.

"Do you know the story about David and Goliath?" Alan whispered.

"You mean the story about David killing Goliath with his slingshot?" Henry whispered back.

"Yeah," Alan said. "But Goliath didn't die. People think he did, but he didn't. He's invincible. He can never die. Nothing can kill him." Alan leaned in even closer. "I'm Goliath. But no one can ever know," he whispered as he fell asleep.

*** CHAPTER 7 ***

The next morning Henry woke Alan and told him he was taking him into Toronto to see his doctor. Henry had called Dr. Sinclair the night before and had him paged through his after-hours emergency service. Sure enough, Dr. Sinclair had called him back within an hour. He normally didn't schedule appointments at his office on Friday but would be at the hospital following up with some of his patients, so he told Henry to bring Alan there around 10AM and he would fit him in.

Grandma was coming with them as well. Henry had indicated he could handle it on his own, but she had insisted and Henry knew it was pointless to argue with her. When Dr. Sinclair came to the waiting room to find them, he said he wanted to spend some time alone with Alan first to assess him. They returned to the waiting room about half an hour later and Alan looked a lot better.

"Could I spend a few minutes with you now to get a more complete picture of Alan's condition?" Dr. Sinclair asked.

"Henry, I think you can explain to the doctor how Alan

was acting yesterday," his mother said. "I really don't think you need me. I think I should stay here with Alan."

"Sure Mom," Henry replied as he followed the doctor back into one of the examination rooms. Henry told the doctor about all of the wild stories that Alan had been telling them the day before.

"That's fairly typical of someone in a manic state," the doctor said. "It appears that he hasn't taken his medications for several days. I just gave him some medication that will hopefully start to stabilize him fairly quickly and then we'll have to get him back on a regular dosage." However, the doctor became much more concerned when Henry told him about Alan's illusion that he was invincible and that he was the giant Goliath from the old David and Goliath story.

"I'm thinking we should admit him for a few days to keep an eye on him," Dr. Sinclair said. "If he's under the delusion of being invincible, I'm afraid he might do something stupid and do some real harm to himself."

"Eileen, can you ask Alan Shaw and his mother to join us in here?" the doctor asked one of the nurses standing behind the desk. "They're out in the waiting room." When they arrived, Dr. Sinclair explained everything to them all. He particularly made sure that Alan understood what was going on.

"I'm sorry for causing so much trouble," Alan said to Henry and his mother when they were getting ready to leave.

"Don't worry about it," Henry said. "I'm sure you'll be back to normal within a few days."

Henry drove his mother back home and then headed into work. He had already missed an important meeting that morning with Greg Blackwood. He knew that family took precedence over work and had already left a voice-mail indicating he wouldn't be able to make the meeting, but he still felt guilty. When he arrived at the office, he headed to Greg Blackwood's office to let him know the situation and apologize for missing the meeting. When he got there, Greg wasn't in his office but he could see him with several associates from the litigation department in the boardroom just down the hall. Since the boardroom had glass walls, Henry could see that the meeting looked like it was wrapping up. Sure enough, Greg saw Henry and gave a signal that he'd be there in five minutes.

Henry headed into Greg's office to wait. Greg's office had numerous bookshelves made of solid mahogany to match the huge desk and was one of the largest offices within the firm, indicative of his importance. Henry had been in Greg's office several times before but this was the first time he noticed a collection of old guns inside glass cases sitting on top of some of the shelves. He was trying to read the inscription on an old musket when Greg walked in.

"I didn't know you were a gun collector," Henry said.

"I'm not," Greg said. "They were my father's and they were left to me when he passed away. Personally, I hate them and I sold or gave away most of them but I decided to keep a few of the real old ones that were most important to him. He knew the history of every gun in his collection and he would spend hours telling me about each one."

"I'm sorry I missed our meeting this morning," Henry said. He explained about the family medical crisis that had occurred, although he left out most of the details.

"I hope your brother will be OK," Greg said. Henry could tell he really meant it.

"You didn't miss much at the meeting this morning. The Finance Committee had a few concerns about our tech budget for the merger, but I convinced them everything was

OK. There's nothing to worry about."

There was a soft knock on the door and Henry turned to see Samuel Richards, one of the founding partners of the firm standing in the doorway. "Congratulations on winning the Westbrook case yesterday," Mr. Richards said. "That was an unexpected win. I hear you were quite impressive in the courtroom." Greg walked over and shook Mr. Richards' hand and whispered something to him.

"You're kidding, but I'm sure you helped him along the path," Mr. Richards said as he gave Greg a pat on the shoulder before continuing on his way.

"So, did you slice and dice some insurance guy on the stand like you normally do?" Henry asked.

"No, I actually lucked out on this one. We couldn't get our hands on any solid evidence to support our claim. No letters we could produce. No chain of emails or voice-mail recordings that would prove that the hospital had screwed up our client's treatment, and that the insurance company knew about it."

"So, how did you win it?" Henry asked.

"I had a sense that one of the Vice Presidents knew the whole story, including the stuff not written down," Greg replied, "so I called him to the stand and only asked him one question."

"*Could you tell me what happened?* was all that I asked him."

"And he spilled the whole thing?"

"Well, he started by just repeating the same lines all of the others had said, almost word for word. I'm sure just like their lawyer had told them to. But when he finished, I didn't ask him another question. I just looked at him. After a dead silence of about 30 seconds, he started telling more. Whenever he would stop, I would just look at him. And then he'd tell more. This happened several times until he'd spilled the whole thing."

"Amazing," Henry said. "Didn't the defence lawyers object?"

"They tried, a few times, but the judge just asked him if he had anything more to add and he'd start talking again. Sometimes you get the sense that someone just wants to do the right thing and all you have to do is stand back and let them do it. I think if I had tried to pull it out of him by badgering him with questions, he would have become defensive and clammed up."

"Brilliant," Henry said as he rose from his chair. "Congratulations," he said, shaking Greg's hand.

As Henry walked down the hall toward his own office, he thought about how well Greg could read people. He was sure he would learn a lot by just knowing him.

*** CHAPTER 8 ***

"Hurry up Dad," David yelled a few days later as he stood waiting for Henry at the front door. "Coach doesn't tolerate anyone being late and I'm already running laps after practice as it is."

"Coming," Henry said as he grabbed his keys from the bowl on the table near the front door.

David threw his soccer bag in the back seat and Henry was just about to back out of the driveway when he saw Alan's car pull in behind him. He jumped out of the car and waved for Alan to pull his car up beside his.

"Hi Alan," Henry said. "I'll be back in a few minutes. I have to drive David to his soccer practice and we're already late."

"Mind if I tag along?" Alan asked as he got out of his car.

"Hop in," Henry said, and Alan crawled into the back seat pushing David's soccer bag to the side.

"You're looking much better," Henry said.

Alan certainly did. Gone were the gold chains and other bling from the pimp getup he was wearing the last time they had seen him. He was talking at a normal pace and volume and not displaying any of the hyper-activity they'd seen before.

"Yeah, they released me from the hospital yesterday, although they don't want me to go back to work until next week. They also want me to start on a regular exercise program. I just met with a personal trainer before coming out to see you." Henry had noticed the track suit that Alan was wearing.

"Hey David," Alan said, reaching forward from the back seat and putting his hand on David's shoulder. "How are things going with you?"

"OK," was all that David said. Henry could tell that David was still uneasy around his uncle. He bolted from the car almost before it had come to a stop when they got to the soccer field. Henry and Alan got out of the car and decided to stay a bit to watch the practice.

"What's up with him?" Alan asked.

Henry hesitated before answering. "He was a little freaked out by your behaviour last week. I think he's a little afraid of you. He's also worried that he's going to end up like you, because we all tell him he looks and acts like you when you were his age. Give him some time. He'll come around."

Alan apologized again. It seemed that's all he'd been doing lately.

"I see you found your car," Henry said. "Where was it?"

"I'd left it at the place where I got the limousine, although I don't remember taking it there. When I checked my voice-mail, there were about twenty voice-mail messages including three from the limousine company asking me to come pick up my car or they were going to have it towed. There were also a bunch of voice-mails from people I don't even know."

Henry and Alan continued to talk. They hadn't realized how long they had been talking until they saw the soccer players starting to gather up their gear as the practice was now over. They walked over towards David. "Ready to go David?"

"Sorry Dad, but I still have to run some laps," David replied as he shot a glance towards his coach.

"Mind if I run with you?" Alan asked. "I'm supposed to start getting some regular exercise."

David shot his dad a nervous look. "It'll be OK David," Henry said, "as long as it's OK with your coach."

"No problem," said the coach.

David and Alan started jogging around the track that circled the soccer pitch, although Henry noted that they seemed to be going much slower than normal. There were a couple of other players who were also running laps, but they were running at a much faster pace so they could get them over with as soon as possible.

As Henry and the coach watched them, the coach came over to talk to Henry. "I didn't really want to have to discipline him," said the coach. "Hell, he won the game for us" he continued, referring to the last game where David had abandoned his normal right-defense position and scored the winning goal. "But I've got to be consistent with everyone on the team. If I let any of them think they can abandon the game plan whenever they feel like it, I'll lose control of the team."

"I understand," Henry said. "And I think he does too."

"I probably should have made some changes to our strategy at half-time. I think a few of the players realized we needed to make a change before I did." The coach paused as he watched David continue around the track. "That's a hell of a kid you got there," he said as he smiled and put his hand on Henry's shoulder. He picked up a large bag of soccer balls, threw them over his shoulder and carried them to his van.

Henry watched David and Alan continue their laps around the track. He wasn't sure how many laps David was supposed to run as part of his discipline, but he was sure they were doing more than necessary. The other kids had completed their laps and headed off quite a while ago. But Henry was pleased to see his son and brother continue to talk to each other. He didn't want that relationship to fall apart.

He watched as they changed from a jog to a sprint from the far side of the track as they raced the last half-lap. They were running neck and neck, although Henry was pretty sure that David was holding back. Sure enough, David kicked it into another gear with about 50 metres to go and left Alan in his dust. When Alan finally reached the finish line gasping for breath, he saw David waiting there for him. David gave his uncle a high-five and they walked off the track together towards Henry.

"I hope you didn't kill him," Henry said as they approached.

"He did OK for an old guy," David said, smirking.

As they drove back to the house, Henry looked at his brother in the rear view mirror. It was good to see him healthy and happy again, albeit tired. When they got back to the house, Alan only stayed for a few minutes. He wanted to pop in to let everyone know he was out of the hospital and OK. He thanked them all for being there when he needed them, and apologized yet again.

Henry stopped by David's room later that night just before he went to bed. "I was glad to see you talking with Uncle Alan today when you were running laps. You were out there a long time. What were you talking about?"

"A bunch of stuff," David said. "He told me about his

bipolar condition and the medications he has to take. He told me about his work and some other stuff he's doing. He said he might need my help with some stuff and asked if he could work out with me sometime."

"It sounds like you're not afraid of him anymore. I'm glad."

"He's still a little weird," David said, "but most old people are."

"I'll try not to take that personally," Henry said as he closed the door. "Goodnight."

*** CHAPTER 9 ***

The computer screen flashed briefly as the laptop was turned on. "Please enter your password:" displayed on the screen and Alan entered the cryptic 24-character password. The usual series of messages displayed.

"Negotiating protocol…."

"Securing communications channel…"

Finally, Alan saw the greeting he was waiting for.

"Welcome, Goliath"

"Retrieve instructions," he typed at the simple ">" prompt.

"No new instructions," the computer displayed after a few seconds. Alan was pleased to see that he hadn't missed anything over the last several days while he was out of commission. He hadn't told Edward Bronson about his bipolar condition and wondered if he suspected anything. Alan knew he had been careless about not keeping up with his medications and he promised himself he wouldn't let it happen again. Their work was too important to let one person mess things up.

Alan remembered the first time he had met Edward

Bronson, almost two years ago. Alan had stayed late at the menswear store to measure Mr. Bronson for a custom-tailored suit and they had immediately hit it off, even though they had entirely different backgrounds. Alan had expressed his frustration with the current politicians and Mr. Bronson shared his frustration.

"I know a lot of these guys personally," said Mr. Bronson. "If you talk to them individually, they have a lot of really good ideas. But as soon as the politics get involved, they become real jerks."

"Egos, money and political ambition have a habit of getting in the way," Alan said.

"I think you're right," said Mr. Bronson.

It was a few weeks after that initial conversation that Mr. Bronson had come to him with an idea. "A few of my newspapers have been working on a story about finding a way to move oil from Canada to the southern U.S. that will have minimal environmental impact. The oil companies want to build a pipeline as that's the cheapest solution but the environmentalists hate that solution because of the damage to the environment if there's a break in the pipeline."

"You mean **when** there's a break in the pipeline," Alan said. "You know it's just a matter of time until there's a break somewhere."

"Precisely – the frustrating thing is that I think we can find a solution that makes everyone happy if we could just get them to work together. The key is that it has to be anonymous. No one gets to patent the solution. No one gets to take credit for coming up with the solution to get elected. We just have to get the smartest people working together on a solution."

"I'd like to help," Alan said, "but I'm not an expert in anything."

"You don't have to be. We'll need a network of couriers to exchange information between those working on a solution. We don't want environmentalists knowing that they're working with engineers from oil companies, or Republicans knowing that they're working with Democrats. As soon as they find out they're working with their arch enemies, everything breaks down. I'll be the only one who knows who's in the network."

It was only a week after that conversation that Mr. Bronson had shown up with a specially modified laptop computer. It had a small device in it that allowed data to be written on tiny digital chips, the same kind used in cameras and cell phones. Mr. Bronson said they needed a way to secretly exchange the information.

"Why don't you just encrypt it and send it over the internet?" Alan asked.

"The internet isn't as anonymous as you think," said Mr. Bronson. "The telecommunication companies can track almost anything these days and are regularly asked to provide their data to authorities. In the U.S., they don't even need a warrant to get the data. All they have to do is say it's a matter of national security."

It was Alan who noted that these chips were small enough to be sewn into clothes, or practically anything else for that matter. And thus, the network was born. It was also Alan who had suggested approaching Frenchie Bouchard to be one of their couriers. He knew that Frenchie travelled around the world on a regular basis as part of his job.

"He might be a little too high profile for us," Mr. Bronson said. "Normally, I'd like our couriers to be less conspicuous and blend into the background and Frenchie is anything but that." But Mr. Bronson agreed to consider it and approached Frenchie a few weeks later after doing a complete background check.

It surprised both of them how quickly their little network grew. It turns out there are lots of people who are willing to work on important problems for the common good with no promise of fame or fortune, almost like a network of "Secret Santa's".

Unfortunately, they would find out that no good deed goes unpunished.

*** CHAPTER 10 ***

There were only a handful of players waiting in front of the
school as the bus that was going to take them to Barrie for
the provincial championships pulled up. It was about
7:15AM and the bus wasn't scheduled to leave for another
fifteen minutes. The first game for the girls' team was at
10AM and the first game for the boys' team was at noon.
After that, it would depend on whether they won or lost the
game.

The coaches opened the luggage compartments on the
side of the bus and started loading in their gear consisting
of soccer balls, pylons, water bottles and medical kits. They
told the players that the girls should load their stuff into the
front compartment and the guys should load their stuff into
the middle compartment. As more players arrived, they had
to be told again and again how things were to be organized.
Despite that, there were still a few who got it wrong.

Although there was no assigned seating on the bus, it
always seemed to follow the same pattern. The two coaches
of the girls' team always sat in the first seat, the girls took
the seats near the front of the bus and the boys grouped

together at the back of the bus. The coaches of the boys' team always seemed to sit around the middle of the bus.

Ashley was one of the first players to board the bus. It was her first year on the girls' soccer team and she was a little smaller than the other girls on the team. Despite that, she was one of the better players on the team, although the other more popular girls seemed to get more credit for the team's success. She had deliberately sat near the middle of the bus and was looking out the bus window when she saw David arrive and throw his gear into the luggage compartment. She flipped her light brown hair and glanced at her reflection in the bus window to make sure she looked her best. Although she knew it wouldn't happen, she hoped that David would sit next to her for the bus ride.

"I guess we've been assigned to room together," Jessica said as she plopped herself down in the seat beside Ashley. "It should be fun." Although Ashley and Jessica had always been friendly towards each other, they were hardly close. It appeared that the room assignments had been done by jersey number, as Jessica was number five and Ashley was number six. Ashley looked up as David was heading down the aisle towards the back of the bus and tried to give him her best smile.

"Hi David," she said as he approached, although Jessica said it at exactly the same time so it sounded like they'd planned it.

"Hi Ashley, Jessica," David said as he headed by them towards the back of the bus.

The coaches were now going through the bus ticking off names to make sure all of the players were on board and the bus pulled out shortly thereafter.

Ashley was starting to pull her iPod out of her coat pocket and was getting ready to put the ear buds in when Jessica leaned in and whispered to her. "Are you and David hooking up?"

"Noooo," she whispered back, feeling her face turn beet red as she said it.

"Well, if you don't have any objections, I'm going to try to hook up with him at the resort this weekend."

Ashley didn't know what to say. "I'm not sure he's your type," she finally said, but even she didn't believe that. Jessica was every guy's type. She was tall, blonde and athletic. She could probably have any guy she wanted. Why had she set her sights on David, the only guy Ashley had ever been interested in?

"Well, you never know until you try," Jessica said. "If you see my hair bandana hooked over the door knob of the room tonight, don't come a-knockin, if you know what I mean, just room with one of the other girls."

"OK, but I don't think…" Ashley started to reply, but Jessica had already bolted from her seat to go sit with one of the other girls. Ashley could feel tears starting to pool in her eyes, so she put her ear buds in and closed her eyes pretending to be listening to music. She wouldn't stand a chance competing against a girl like Jessica. She was still emotionally frayed when the bus got to the soccer fields in Barrie.

The girls' team lost their first game that morning and Ashley hadn't played very well at all. She'd lost her focus and to be honest, she didn't care. They'd have to win their next two matches to have any chance of winning the provincial championship.

Ashley stayed around to watch the boys game and they had won their game quite easily, having taken a three-nothing lead in the first half and adding a fourth goal near the end of the game. Jessica had also stayed to watch the boys' game and Ashley could see her down there on the sidelines flirting with David as they walked off the field at the end of the game.

When they got to the resort later in the afternoon, there was general chaos as all of the players from all of the teams tried to find their rooms. The resort consisted of a main lodge which had the reception area, a large games room with video games, pool and ping pong tables, and a very large dining area that could accommodate all of the players from all of the teams. The main lodge had a few rooms, although most of the rooms were located in numerous lodges scattered throughout the property with the lodges named after the different types of trees. The boys' team from their school were all located in the Birch lodge and David was pleased to see that he would be sharing his room with Alex. The rooms of the girls' team were all located in the Oak lodge.

It was great having all of the players from all of the teams together for meals. Although they were competing against each other, it was nice to get to know the other players off of the field. Most of the players congregated in the games room after supper and Ashley had gone there as well, but wasn't feeling very sociable.

"Don't worry about it," Ashley's coach said as she sat down beside her. She had noticed Ashley sitting by herself. "I'm sure you'll play much better in the next game." Ashley nodded, but didn't really respond. "This is quite a nice facility," the coach continued. "You should try out some of the games."

"I will," Ashley said, giving a fake smile. Then the coach headed off to join a ping pong game with a few of the other coaches.

Ashley continued to watch David who was playing pool with Alex but when she returned after going to the washroom, she saw that the teams had changed and it was now David and Jessica taking on two players from another school. She could see that Jessica was now in full flirt mode and couldn't bear to watch any more.

Ashley wandered down to the other end of the games room and watched several other students playing Texas hold'em poker. They weren't allowed to play for real money and didn't even have real chips, but they had raided the children's crafts cupboard and were using Lego pieces as chips. Ashley didn't really understand the game, but it was easy to see that one of the coaches was winning as he had so many Lego pieces in front of him that he'd started building some sort of a high-rise apartment building out of them. "So young, so much to learn," the coach would say every time he won another hand.

Ashley continued wandering around the games room. Some people were playing other games like Risk or Monopoly, but most of the students were just sitting around in groups talking. No one was talking about soccer.

"Curfew in half an hour," shouted one of the coaches from the other end of the room.

Ashley scanned the room which had thinned out considerably, even before the coach's announcement about the pending curfew. There were still a few people playing pool, but she didn't see David or Jessica. She hadn't seen them for a while.

Ashley started to walk over to the Oak lodge with several of her teammates, who each headed into their rooms. Ashley's room was at the end and her heart sank when she saw Jessica's red hair bandana hanging over the door knob. She tip-toed towards the door and her heart sank even more when she heard the sounds coming from the room. Once again, she could feel tears start to well up in her eyes. She didn't know what to do or where to go. She didn't want to go to one of the other girl's rooms because she didn't want them to see her this way. She tip-toed away from the room and was wandering among the various lodges when she saw a couple of people coming out the back door of the main lodge. She didn't know them, but they held the door open for her as she approached. When she got inside, she realized this was the back door exit of the games room, which was now deserted. She slumped down on a couch along the hallway just inside the door. She was trying not to cry, but failing. She lay down on the couch and continued to cry until she fell asleep.

* * *

"I gotta go," David said. "It's almost curfew." David had been hanging out with several friends from the resort, people he had worked with at the lodge over the summer. It was good connecting with them again and finding out what everyone was up to. Most of them were in university now, although a few were still in high school, but all were pleased to have been called in to work on the weekend to pick up a few extra bucks.

It was only a few minutes to curfew and David determined he'd have to take a shortcut and head out through the back door of the games room in order to make it to his room in the Birch lodge by the time the coach came around to check on them. As he headed down the hallway, he was surprised to see a girl lying on the couch. He was even more surprised to see that it was Ashley.

"What are you doing out here?" David whispered as he knelt beside the couch and touched Ashley on the arm.

She woke with a start and it took her a few seconds to figure out her surroundings. "I didn't want to bother you and Jessica," she said, not having the courage to look him in the eye. She also didn't want him to see that she had been crying.

"Me and Jessica?" David asked, looking confused.

"What are you talking about?"

"Jessica's hooking up with someone in our room," Ashley said. "I thought it was you."

"She's not my type," David said. "Come on, we've got to get you another room. If the coaches catch us out past curfew, there will be hell to pay." David took her hand and helped her up off the couch. Ashley desperately tried to wipe the tears from her face with her other hand. She was sure she looked like a wreck.

They headed back to the front desk and David asked the clerk if they could get another room for Ashley, offering only a weak explanation that she'd had a tiff with her assigned roommate. David read the name Malcolm on the clerk's nametag, but he didn't know him at all because he'd never worked with him.

"I wish I could help you," Malcolm said, "but we're completely booked."

David stood there, trying to figure out what to do next. He noticed Bryan, one of the other clerks, gesturing with his eyes to meet him over by the brochure stand. Bryan worked the night shift and David had worked with him over the past summer. Bryan was usually coming off shift when David was starting his shift. Bryan picked up a stack of brochures and headed over to the brochure stand where he pretended to be restocking the various sections. When David came over, Bryan pulled a room key from between the brochures and slipped it to David.

"You can probably use Pine-14," he whispered to David. "We can't rent it out because they're replacing the tiles in the shower. The room is fine and the bathroom is OK too, but you won't be able to use the shower. If you want, you can use the showers by the pool."

"Thanks," David said. "I owe you one."

David headed back over to Ashley, took her hand and

told her he would take her to another room explaining everything should be good except for the shower. They would have to be careful not to be seen as they were now well past curfew, but David knew the way to get there while staying off the main pathways. When they got to the room, David unlocked the door and noticed that the room was a bit cold, so he turned on the heat by adjusting the controls which were hidden behind the dresser.

"The room should warm up in a few minutes," David said.

David went into the bathroom and saw a stack of tiles and grouting tools on the floor, so he pushed them back out of the way. He flushed the toilet and made sure everything except the shower was working. There were no towels in the bathroom but he knew they usually kept some extra towels in the closet and was pleased to see they were there.

"Pretty much as advertised," David said. "Are you going to be OK?" He could sense that Ashley was a little apprehensive. "I can stay if you want and sleep on the couch," he said, glancing toward the couch facing the TV at the other side of the room.

"I don't want to get you into any trouble. You've already done so much to help me."

"No problem. What's the worst they could do to me?" David said, although he didn't even want to think about how much trouble they'd be in if the coaches found out.

"We better get some sleep," David said. "We've both got early games tomorrow."

Ashley headed into the washroom as David pulled some extra blankets from the clothes closet he'd seen there when he was looking for towels.

Ashley looked at herself in the bathroom mirror and was disappointed at how she looked. She washed the mascara from her face which had been smeared by her crying. She didn't have a comb but managed to make her hair look better with just her fingers. Not great, but a thousand percent better she thought to herself. She debated whether to take off her jeans, but decided to chance it when she realized her top came down far enough to cover all of the essentials.

When she emerged from the bathroom, she saw David curled up looking extremely uncomfortable on the couch. It was more of a love-seat than a couch, so there was no way that David was going to fit on it. "You can sleep in the bed if you want," Ashley suggested. "I trust you."

"Yeah, I'm not sure I'd be able to move tomorrow if I slept on this thing," David said. He started pulling the multitude of extra pillows that were on the bed and placing them like a wall down the middle of the bed. He'd always hated those extra pillows as they seemed to have no useful purpose, other than for decoration. Finally, he'd found a use for them. He pulled a couple of more pillows from the couch and added them to the wall.

"How's that?" David asked.

"That's fine," Ashley said, "but it's not really necessary. I trust you." However, she wasn't sure she trusted herself. Ashley turned off the lamp and crawled into her side of the bed. The room was almost completely dark except for the moonlight that shone through a slight opening in the curtains. David stripped down to his boxer shorts and crawled into his side of the bed. They laid there facing each other, but separated by a wall of pillows. They both wanted to say something, but didn't know what to say. It seemed like an eternity until Ashley spoke.

"I'm glad it wasn't you that was with Jessica," she said, placing her hand on the top of the mountain of pillows.

"I told you she's not my type," David answered,

reaching his arm over the mountain of pillows and taking her hand.

"Goodnight," he said. "Pleasant dreams."

"Goodnight," she answered. She was already living her dream.

* * *

When the first beam of light came streaming through the small opening in the curtains, Ashley woke to find her head laying half on David's chest, with her arm hugging him like he was a teddy bear from her childhood. Gone was the mountain of pillows that had been between them. She raised her head slightly to see that most of the pillows had been pushed to the bottom of the bed and a few had fallen to the floor. She wasn't sure whether David had moved the pillows or whether she'd done it herself subconsciously while she slept. But she was happy either way.

"Good morning," whispered David. Ashley hadn't realized he was awake until he spoke.

"It looks like your wall of pillows somehow came tumbling down in the middle of the night," Ashley said.

"Yeah, I don't think I'll ever be an architect," David said, kissing her lightly on her forehead.

"I think you can be whatever you want to be," Ashley said, pulling herself up so she was half on top of David and looking deeply into his eyes. She was looking for more than just a little kiss on the forehead. Ashley had always been somewhat shy as a girl and really only spoke when spoken to, but she was suddenly feeling much more aggressive. She kissed him full on the mouth.

Suddenly there was a knock on the door and they both froze. "Breakfast is in twenty minutes," said a voice from outside. Ashley remained frozen in fear wondering who knew they were in there. But David had recognized Bryan's voice. He slid from the bed and opened the door a crack, but Bryan had already gone.

"We'd better get up and get out of here," David whispered. "I don't want to get Bryan into any trouble for letting us use this room." David headed into the bathroom while Ashley got out of bed and slipped on her jeans.

"Your turn," David said, when he emerged from the bathroom. "I'll straighten up the room."

When Ashley looked at herself in the bathroom mirror, she could still see the passion in her eyes. She'd never felt like this before and it both excited and scared her. Who knows what they would have done if they hadn't been interrupted by the knock on the door. Surely one of them would have kept things under control, but she wasn't sure she would have, which scared her even more. She wondered if David was having the same feelings, but her thoughts started drifting into doubt the more she thought about it. Maybe it had been her that had subconsciously knocked down the wall of pillows that had been between them. Maybe David was just being a nice guy and helping her out when she had no place to stay for the night. She knew David liked her, but did he **really** like her? He had simply kissed her on the forehead. She had been the one who had practically jumped on top of him. "Oh my God," she thought.

"We better get going," David said, tapping lightly on the outside of the bathroom door.

Ashley wondered how long she'd been in the bathroom having her mini panic attack. When she emerged from the bathroom, she was surprised to see that David had stripped the sheets from the bed and was holding them in his hand. He'd put the bedspread back on the bed and laid the pillows out exactly as they were originally. The room looked like it hadn't been used at all. David reached into the bathroom and grabbed the towels from the rack. He put the shower tiles and the grouting equipment back where it had been when they arrived the night before.

"We can't be seen leaving together," David whispered as he opened the door a crack to see if anyone was outside.

He could see some girls a few doors down getting ready to leave their rooms to head over for breakfast. Further down, he could see a laundry cart as the maids were now starting their rounds. He saw the last girl emerge from her door and join the group as they started to walk away.

"OK, I think you can go now," David whispered.

"Thanks for helping me out," Ashley said as she started to slip out the door. This time it was her who gave David a little kiss on the forehead. David pulled her back into the room, pressed her up against the wall and kissed her full on the mouth, hard.

"OK, go," he said as he opened the door again. Ashley scurried to catch up to the group of girls that had just left. Although they were from another team and she didn't know any of them, she felt she'd be less conspicuous if she appeared to be part of their group. As she walked behind them, she felt almost like skipping. That kiss had told her what she needed to know. David **really** did like her.

David watched as the group of girls walked away out of sight. The maid was pulling some clean towels from her cart. When she went into the room two doors down, David emerged from his room and dropped his soiled sheets and towels into her laundry cart as he walked by.

When David reached the main lodge, he slipped Bryan the room key as he walked by the reception desk and continued into the main dining room, which was now almost completely full with the soccer players getting breakfast. He saw Ashley sitting at a large table on the other side of the room with her teammates. They made brief eye contact before Ashley turned her head to join the conversation at her table.

David was pleased to see Alex heading up to the buffet. David grabbed a plate and slid in behind him in the line.

"Good morning," Alex said, "and how was your night?"

David ignored the question. "Does coach know I wasn't there last night?" David asked.

"I don't think so," Alex said. "I told him you were in the bathroom when he knocked on the door to do the curfew check last night. I think he believed me."

"Thanks," David said. "I owe you one."

"Is everything OK?" Alex asked, continuing to fish for details.

"Perfect," David replied, "and that's all I'm saying."

*** CHAPTER 11 ***

Ashley's soccer team played much better in their game that morning, but still only managed to play to a one-one draw. They would have to win their next game by a large margin to have any hope of making it to tomorrow's final, and they would have to have the teams ahead of them in the standings lose their last game in the preliminary round. Ashley had played a much better game this time. Her coach and several of her teammates had noticed that she had a lot more jump in her game today, rather than the down-in-the-dumps attitude they'd seen the day before.

"You seem to have gotten out of the right side of the bed this morning," her coach said as they walked off of the field. "We'll need that kind of energy in our next game."

"Thanks," Ashley said. Her coach didn't realize how close to the truth she really was.

David's team also played well in their match that morning, edging their opponent out by a two-one score. David had seen his dad and grandmother arrive in the stands just before the game had started. They hadn't come to the game yesterday because Henry was tied up at work and couldn't get away. They came down to the field level to congratulate David when the game was over.

"Great game," Henry said. "I saw on the notice-board that you guys won your game yesterday as well."

"Thanks Dad, although we still have to win the next one to guarantee a place in the Championship game tomorrow."

"You played so well," his grandmother said, giving him a hug.

Ashley had also come over to congratulate David, although she was hovering in the background. She had only seen the last few minutes of David's game as her own game had been playing on an adjacent field at the same time.

"How did your game go?" David asked when he saw her.

"We tied," Ashley replied.

They all walked together back to the small clubhouse which had the change-rooms and a large board showing the game results and standings. Ashley headed off to join the rest of her teammates.

"Ashley seems nice," Grandma said to David.

"She's just a friend," David said, knowing that his grandmother was fishing about a potential budding relationship between them.

"Please dear," Grandma replied. "I wasn't born yesterday."

In the matches later that afternoon, Ashley's team had once again tied their game so their record of a loss and two ties meant they were eliminated from the girls' championship game on Sunday. David's team won their afternoon match and would now be playing in the boys' championship game against a team from North Bay.

Since the girls' team had been eliminated, some of the girls would be heading home with their parents. Those who wanted to stay would be returning to the resort on the team bus. Since Ashley's parents hadn't come to the matches, Henry had offered to drive Ashley back home with them. However, the coaches had indicated they were only allowed to let a player return early if their parents signed a release form. Although Ashley had thanked David's dad for the offer, she was pleased that she would be spending another night at the resort. She was hoping things would pick up where they had left off the previous night.

"We'll be back for the championship game tomorrow," Henry said to David while standing outside the team bus. "Uncle Alan said he might come as well, but you never know with him."

"Thanks for coming to the game," David said, giving both his dad and his grandma a hug. He watched them head off toward their car before he boarded the team bus.

When David boarded the bus, he noticed the front part of the bus was almost empty as there were only about five or six girls that were returning to the resort. The rest had headed home with their parents. The back of the bus was filled with the boys' team who seemed much louder than normal in their excitement about making it to the championship game. David noticed Ashley sitting alone about half-way back on the bus. As he started the walk toward the back of the bus, he stopped at Ashley's seat.

"This seat taken?" he asked as he threw his jacket on the seat.

Ashley beamed when he sat down beside her. They didn't really say much to each other as they both put their ear buds in and turned on their iPods to listen to music during the drive to the resort. They hoped no one noticed when they secretly held hands underneath David's jacket that lay between them.

But the coach had noticed. He wasn't born yesterday either.

* * *

The dining room at the resort had a different feel to it when the players from the various teams gathered for supper that night as there was much more tension in the air. The players from David's team eyed the players from the North Bay team and they were doing the same in return. You could tell they were each assessing each other.

"Boy, those guys are huge," Alex said to David as he scanned the players sitting at the North Bay table. "They must put something in the water up in North Bay."

"The bigger they are, the harder they fall," David said. "Number 18 is their leading scorer. Do you know which one he is?"

"I think he's the one second from the end," Alex said. "He's the one that looks like he's grown a full beard since breakfast."

They hadn't played each other in the preliminary rounds, but both teams had won all of their games. The North Bay team had won their games by quite a margin.

The tension continued in the games room that evening. Even players from teams that had already been eliminated from the championship game seemed to have a bit of chip on their shoulder. A couple of players from an Ottawa team that had been beaten soundly by the North Bay team had come up to David to offer suggestions on strategy and to wish them well in the championship game.

"Number 16, the blonde guy, is the playmaker," one of the Ottawa players had told him. "If you go for the ball when he has it, he can make you look real stupid. So, stay back on him and let him make the first move. He's always looking to make a pass so don't worry about him shooting. Number 18 is their finisher. He plays real physical. He'd rather run over you than around you. Good luck tomorrow. I hope you guys win."

"I hope you fucking kill them," said another player from the Ottawa team who had been listening to the conversation. He was sporting a large bruise on his cheek which he had received from number 18.

The number of players in the games room was starting to thin out. David and Alex decided to head off to their room in the Birch lodge. However, when they were heading out of the main lodge, David saw Ashley sitting alone on one of the benches on the veranda.

"I'll catch up with you," David said to Alex as he headed over towards Ashley.

Her eyes lit up as she saw him approach. "Jessica headed home with her parents after the game today so I'm alone in my room in the Oak lodge," whispered Ashley, pausing at the end trying to gauge David's reaction. "Just saying..."

David knew exactly what she was saying. "I don't think I can chance it," David said. "It's the championship game tomorrow and I'd get suspended if we got caught." He sensed Ashley's disappointment. "It's not that I don't want to," he continued.

"I know," Ashley sighed. "You're probably right."

"Curfew is in 25 minutes," said a loud voice coming from behind them. It was his coach. He was making his announcement to the dozen or so students who were hovering outside the main lodge, but David noticed he was looking right at him when he said it.

"Good luck tomorrow," Ashley said, giving David's hand a squeeze before she started walking away towards her lodge.

David turned and walked towards his coach. "Big game tomorrow - I'll be sure to get a good night's sleep."

"And don't be in the bathroom again tonight when I do

my curfew check," said the coach.

* * *

The next day, the stands were about half full at the championship game as both teams were going through their warm-ups, although there was a steady stream of people still arriving. David was pleased to see his dad and his grandmother already seated up near the back of the stands and he waved to them when he saw them. David knew his dad liked sitting near the top of the stands so he could better see plays develop across the entire field.

David saw his uncle Alan climbing the stairs towards where they were sitting. He was pleased to see his uncle had come, although he still felt a little uneasy around him since his meltdown several weeks ago. David had tried to be friendly toward his uncle, mostly to please his dad, but he was also a little intrigued by him. Uncle Alan was full of interesting stories, although David suspected most only existed in his fantasy bipolar world.

David also saw Ashley sitting with some other girls directly behind the players' bench. He headed over and took a swig from his water bottle, but he wasn't really thirsty. It was just an excuse so he could say hello to Ashley.

The coach called all of the players over and told the players to take off their practice jerseys and put on their game jerseys. David could sense that his teammates were all quite nervous as there wasn't the normal amount of pre-game chatter. Since this was the championship game, they had been told to line up on either side of midfield as all of the players would be introduced. The North Bay players were introduced first and there were small cheers as each player's name came over the loudspeakers. You could tell where each player's family and friends were sitting because that's where each cheer would be the loudest. David waited for his name to be called as they announced each of his teammates going in order of their jersey number.

"Number 14, David Shaw," said the voice over the loudspeaker. David took one step forward and did a small wave to the stands. There was a small cheer from the stands, but David could hear his Uncle Alan's voice over them all.

"Number 15, Alex B...." and there was a pause by the announcer. The team started to chuckle because they all knew who's name the announcer was struggling to pronounce. He wasn't the first and he wouldn't be the last person to have trouble pronouncing it.

"B-B-Budge-ace-zeck," he finally spit out.

"Bee-a-chuck," the team shouted in unison, continuing to laugh.

Alex's last name was spelled B-u-j-a-c-z-e-k and he was always amazed that no one seemed to know how to pronounce it. Although Alex was slightly embarrassed, the incident seemed to remove all of the tension in the team. The normal pre-game chatter and joking around had now returned.

Once the game started, the North Bay team had the Warriors on the defensive from the opening whistle. They scored on a corner kick about 10 minutes into the game when number 18 basically ran over Alex and headed the ball into the net. The Warriors screamed for a foul to be called but the referee ignored their complaints. Worse still, Alex had been injured on the play and was now limping noticeably. The coach offered to take Alex out of the game, but he refused and told the coach he thought he could play through it.

During a stoppage in play, the coach called David and Alex to the sidelines. "How's your leg?" the coach asked.

"OK," Alex said. The coach realized Alex was lying but knew he wasn't going to leave the game as long as he could walk.

"David, I want you to play man-on-man on number 18, regardless of where he goes on the field," the coach said. "Alex, you move to right defence and let me know if your leg gets worse. And tell Michael I want him to move from mid-field back to help out on defence."

David knew he was in for a challenge. David's advantage had always been his speed and he was significantly faster than number 18, but David was basically skin and bones and this opponent out-weighed him by at least thirty pounds. As the game continued, David found himself getting pushed around. But he refused to back down, despite receiving numerous elbows to the ribs. He was now giving as good as he was getting and they had both been warned by the referee about the physical play.

The North Bay team had lost some of their momentum as David had pretty much removed their finisher from any further scoring chances. However, the Warriors hadn't shown much offence themselves so remained down by a goal at the half.

As David sat on the bench at half-time, he lifted his jersey to see several bruises on his ribs. They hurt a little now but he knew they would hurt significantly more later. Several of his teammates came over and patted him on the shoulder and told him to keep up to the good play. The coach decided to pull Alex from the game at half-time as his limp was getting worse and worse. They felt like they were in a war.

About ten minutes into the second half, David was given a vicious elbow to the side of the head which sent him to the ground. "What the fuck was that?" David said as he got up and pushed his opponent square in the chest, sending him flying backwards and onto his ass. It was hard to tell who was more surprised. David didn't know he had that kind of strength. The referee gave them both yellow cards.

After that, number 18 wasn't nearly as physical. David wasn't sure if it was because he had stood up to him or whether he was afraid of getting another card, which would mean he'd be kicked out of the game. However, the Warriors couldn't seem to mount an attack to get the tying goal. When the final whistle blew, they all slumped to the field, but it was hard to tell whether it was from disappointment or just sheer exhaustion. It seemed to take them forever to take off their cleats and shin pads after the game was over. Many of the players just sat on the bench staring into the sky wondering if there was anything they could have done differently.

"David, Alex, could I talk to you for a few minutes?" shouted the coach who was standing with two other men over near the fence.

David and Alex looked at each other wondering what this was about, but got up and hobbled over to where they were standing. When they got there, the coach introduced them to the two strangers and then left them to talk to each other.

"Great game," said one of the men.

"Yeah, but we lost," replied both David and Alex, almost in unison.

"We've been watching both of you throughout this tournament," he continued. "We've been impressed by your speed and your skills, but we both liked how you didn't back down when the play got more physical."

"Thanks," they replied.

The other fellow now spoke. "We'd like you both to come out for a camp we're holding for the Under-19 National Team," he said.

David and Alex looked at each other, both wide-eyed in amazement. "Sure," they both said, although they still really didn't understand it all. The two men each handed them their business cards and said they'd be contacting them within a few weeks with more details.

As David and Alex headed back to their bench, the coach was waiting for them with a big smile on his face. "Congratulations guys," he said. "They've been scouting you for a while. I'm glad it worked out for both of you."

The coach announced to the rest of the team that David and Alex had been asked to try out for the Under-19 National Team, and all of their teammates came over to offer their congratulations. Suddenly, losing the provincial championship game didn't seem so important.

As David headed off the field, Ashley came running towards him and gave him a big hug. She felt him wince in pain. "Sorry," she said, lifting his jersey to see several bruises. "Oh my God, what did he do to you?"

"I'm OK," David said, "but I think I need another hug." Ashley gave him another hug, but a lighter one this time. "Perfect," David said, dropping his soccer bag and hugging her back.

"I gotta go," Ashley said, looking over her shoulder and seeing that the bus was getting ready to leave. "See you at school tomorrow."

David saw his dad, grandma and Uncle Alan waiting over by the gate. When he got there, he showed them the business cards and told them that both he and Alex had been asked to try out for the U19 National Team.

"Good for you," Henry said.

His grandmother seemed more concerned about his bruises. "They play awfully rough," she said.

"Boy, the National Team," said Uncle Alan. "I always knew you'd be on the world stage at some point."

*** CHAPTER 12 ***

Alan quietly clicked the keys on his laptop computer.

"Welcome, Goliath"

"Retrieve instructions," he typed at the simple ">" prompt.

"Package to be delivered to New York," the computer displayed after a few seconds. As expected, a tiny icon appeared in the lower right portion of the screen.

When Alan clicked on the icon, a small door opened on the side of the computer and a tray slid out. But this was not to load a CD – it was much too small. Alan opened his desk drawer and pulled a tiny plastic object from a box containing a dozen or so similar objects. He carefully inserted the object onto the tray and pushed it back into the computer.

"Package created," the computer displayed on the screen after a few seconds and the small door opened so that Alan could retrieve it from the tray. He carefully placed it in a small plastic bag for protection and then placed it in a small compartment in his wallet. He had no idea what was in the package, but that was not his job. His responsibility was simply to prepare it for transportation. The person that received the package would require their own device and password to decrypt the contents of the package. Alan knew exactly who he would have to contact to deliver the package to New York.

* * *

Henry awoke when his plane touched down in Chicago on Monday morning. He normally couldn't sleep on planes but he'd been burning the candle at both ends lately and the brief catnap he'd had on the short flight from Toronto to Chicago did him a world of good.

He would be in Chicago for the next three days as there was a lot of work to do with various software upgrades. When he got to the Chicago office, two of the vendors who were doing the upgrades were waiting for him when he arrived. They would be the ones doing the actual hands-on work, but it was up to Henry to make sure that any roadblocks were cleared and they didn't get in each other's way during the process. These guys weren't cheap so it was important that they completed their work as quickly as possible.

Henry checked on both of them at lunch, but they were both locked into their tasks and didn't want to take a break. He had the impression that these guys actually preferred eating pizza while sitting at their keyboards anyway. Since things were going well, Henry decided to head out to grab a sandwich at the local Subway outlet. He decided to sit on the concrete edge of one of the many flower stands and eat outside. He was not alone as it was a beautiful day and with the cold weather fast approaching, there wouldn't be many more warm days like today before the snow flew. It was no coincidence that he happened to be sitting outside of the Tribune Tower. He had come here many times since running into Samantha, but had not seen her since. He hoped he would see her and Tammy heading out for lunch someday, but there had been no such luck.

Henry had just finished eating and was getting ready to head back to work when he saw Samantha emerge from the Tribune Tower. He was pretty sure she saw him, but she just kept walking like she was going somewhere important. Henry debated running after her, but decided against it. He checked his watch and noticed it was 12:30 and decided to get back to his own office.

It was no coincidence that Henry was at the exact same spot the next day at 12:30 when Samantha emerged from the building. He knew for sure that she saw him this time because he saw her pause debating whether to come over. He pretended to be reading a newspaper that he had brought along with him that day, but he wasn't fooling anyone.

"You wouldn't be stalking me, would you?" Samantha asked as she leaned against the concrete flowerbed beside him.

"It's just such a nice day to be outside," Henry replied, ignoring her question.

Samantha paused before continuing the conversation. "I suggested that she might want to see you again, but she says she's not ready." Samantha smiled at Henry. "She's going through some things right now."

"Anything I can help with?" Henry asked, fishing for any kind of clue. Samantha seemed to be pondering her answer which gave Henry some hope, but that was quickly shattered.

"Not right now," she said. "I gotta go," she said as she walked away.

Henry was back at the same place at the same time the next day when Samantha emerged from the Tribune Tower. This time she headed directly over to talk to him. "It's amazing the weather we're having," Henry said to her as she approached. "This has been three great days in a row."

"Come with me," Samantha said as she grabbed Henry's hand. Henry followed her, but had no idea where she was taking him. "She's in the hospital," Samantha said as they walked.

"Is she OK?"

"No," replied Samantha, but that was all that she said.

Henry wanted to just drill her with questions, but thought of the advice he had received from Greg Blackwood. "Sometimes you get the sense that a person wants to tell you something and all you have to do is stand back and let them tell it," he recalled. Henry didn't say a word.

"She's going to absolutely kill me," Samantha said, trying to relieve her own guilt. "But I can't seem to get through to her and I think she needs your help." Samantha stopped walking and looked at Henry. "She has breast cancer," she said, seeming relieved that she'd finally gotten it out. She turned and continued to walk. "She had a mastectomy several weeks ago. The surgery went very well and they think she's going to fully recover, but she's not doing very well psychologically right now. That's normal, given the situation, but she's refusing any counseling and she seems to be getting more and more depressed. I visit her every day and she's getting worse and worse and I don't know what to do." Henry and Samantha continued to walk. "That's why she picked you up in the airport that day," Samantha continued. "She's convinced herself that no man is ever going to look at her the same way from now on. She wanted one last time where she knew she was sexually desirable. I tried to talk her out of it. Now she's convinced herself that no man will ever want her again."

Henry could see the tears start to stream down Samantha's cheeks. Samantha stopped walking and seemed to be steeling herself for what she was about to say next. "So, have you got the balls to help her out or are you going to cut and run?"

"I'll help in whatever way I can," Henry said, "but I have no idea what to do."

"Neither do I," Samantha replied, "but we're here."

Henry knew they had been walking for a while but had no idea where they were. He looked up and saw they were standing in front of the hospital.

"Ready?" Samantha asked.

"Wait," Henry said. "What's her real name?"

"Laura," Samantha replied. "Laura Walsh."

Henry went with Samantha into the hospital, but they didn't say anything more to each other as they rode the elevator up to the eight floor. Samantha was deep in thought worrying about how Laura would react when she revealed to her that she'd spilled everything to Henry. Henry was anxious to see her again, but also worried about how she would feel about his presence.

When they stepped off of the elevator, Samantha led the way as she knew where Laura's room was. She had been coming to see her faithfully every day since the surgery. However, when they got to her room the only person there was an attendant who was changing the bedding and cleaning the room.

"I sent them down to the library while I cleaned their room," said the attendant when she saw them standing at the door. The attendant didn't know which of the two patients of the semi-private room Henry and Samantha were there to see, but it didn't matter since she'd sent them both to the same place. This was part of the normal routine for this ward. The attendant could have easily cleaned their room without them leaving, but they used whatever excuse they could to get the patients up and moving on a regular basis.

Samantha led the way to the library, but then stopped and told Henry he should probably wait until she'd told Laura that she'd brought Henry with her. It seemed like an eternity until Samantha came back for him, but in reality it was only a couple of minutes.

"Good luck," Samantha said as she pointed the way to the library at the end of the hall.

When Henry arrived at the door, he realized they were making very liberal use of the word "library". Sure, there was a bookshelf with some books stacked neatly inside, but there were only about 40 books in total, and that was a generous estimate. There were a few tables with magazines scattered on them, a couple of leather loveseats and a few other chairs that looked like standard hospital issue and hard as rock.

Henry scanned the room but didn't see Laura. To his right was a little old lady huddled in a dark blue housecoat that had seen better days. In the middle of the room were two patients sitting at a table playing cribbage. A nurse was sitting in one of the leather loveseats drinking coffee and mindlessly turning the pages of a People magazine. The only other person in the room was a tall woman staring out of the window at the far end of the room. Henry didn't think it was Laura but couldn't be certain as she had her back to him. But this woman had blonde hair, so he wondered if Laura had somehow slipped out of the room before he got there.

"She shouldn't have made you come to see me," said a voice that Henry recognized immediately.

He looked down and suddenly realized the little old lady wasn't a little old lady after all, but Laura. He would never have recognized her except for the voice. She seemed so much smaller than the last time he'd seen her. She was all huddled up as if she was outside in a major snowstorm trying to shield herself from the cold and the elements. Her hair was a muddled tangle of knots that hid her face almost entirely. And she seemed focused on Henry's shoes.

"She didn't **make** me come," Henry said. "I've been desperate to see you again. I've pretty much been stalking Samantha for the last several weeks, waiting outside of the Tribune building hoping to run into both of you."

He paused, hoping to get a response, but got nothing. "I think of you constantly and couldn't bear the thought that I might not ever see you again," Henry continued. "It didn't help that I didn't know your real name until today."

But again, he got no response, not even an acknowledgement. He felt like one of those people who talk to people in comas hoping they can actually hear them, but not really sure. Henry just kept talking and talking, not knowing what else to do. He talked about the warm weather spell they were currently having. He talked about the sad state of the library they were sitting in. He talked about his work and the merger his firm was going through. But Henry was getting nothing back from Laura, nothing at all. She had built a wall around her. When Henry finally ran out of things to talk about, he reached out and took Laura's hand to say goodbye.

"Please don't come back," Laura said, suddenly breaking her silence.

"Sorry," Henry said as he kissed her hand softly. "I don't give up that easily."

Henry found Samantha waiting for him at the elevators. "Well?" she said as he approached.

"We've got our work cut out for us," Henry said as they got into the elevator.

Henry checked his watch as they were walking out of the front door of the hospital and saw that it was almost 3PM.

"I completely lost track of the time," Henry said, waving to a taxi that was waiting in the queue outside of the hospital. "I have to get back to work or else I'm going to get fired. Want to ride back together?"

Samantha nodded as she walked around to the driver's side and slid into the backseat.

"How long has she been like this?" Henry asked, picking up the conversation.

"When she was first diagnosed, she showed almost no emotion at all," Samantha replied. "She researched all of the treatment options and survival rates herself, almost like she was just doing research for one of her stories. The doctors said they believed they had caught the cancer in the first stage and they were only recommending a partial mastectomy, but Laura wanted them to do a total mastectomy. She said something about having an aunt that had gone through the same thing. Apparently, her aunt didn't treat it aggressively enough and it ended up costing her her life."

Henry didn't respond, but seemed deep in thought.

"She was totally logical up until just a few days before the surgery, almost like it was happening to someone else," Samantha continued. "Then a few days before the surgery, she said she wanted to have one last fling, which is when she met you. She was in a totally positive state of mind when she went into surgery, but it was almost like a different person came out of the operating room than who went in."

The taxi pulled up in front of the Tribune Tower and Henry got out to let Samantha out on his side of the car. "I'm supposed to fly back to Toronto tonight," Henry said, "but I'm going to see if I can stay a few more days. I'll try to go see her again tomorrow after work."

"That would be great," Samantha said. "I usually try to

see her on my lunch break and then again in the evening."

Samantha gave Henry a hug and then started to walk towards the building. Henry climbed back in the taxi and gave the driver the address for the law firm's Chicago office.

When Henry finally got back into the office, he discovered that the first vendor had successfully completed his software upgrades and had already left. However, the second vendor had encountered problems and was at a loss as to what to do next.

"Long lunch?" Sharon said when she saw Henry arrive back in the office. Sharon was the Systems Manager for the Chicago office. Henry had already determined that she was totally competent, but he sensed there was a bit of resentment from her that she now reported to him instead of directly to the partners. Henry ignored the shot about taking a long lunch, realizing she had a legitimate complaint.

"Give me ten minutes to reschedule my flight," Henry said, "and then we'll gather together in the small meeting room to figure out what to do."

Henry's first call was to home and was pleased when his mother answered. "Hi Mom - We've run into some problems here in Chicago so I won't be coming back tonight. I probably won't be back until Friday night. Can you watch the boys for me for a few more days?"

"No problem," said his mother. "They pretty much take care of themselves, but I'll make sure they get fed and behave themselves." Henry thanked his mother and placed a quick call to the airline and changed his flight for that evening to a flight on Friday night.

When Henry walked into the small meeting room, Sharon and Dan were waiting for him. Dan was in his early twenties and fresh out of school. He had only worked for the vendor for a few months and this was the first software upgrade and conversion that he had done entirely on his own. He was obviously embarrassed that things hadn't gone as expected as he started apologizing as soon as he saw Henry.

"We'll figure it out," Henry said, trying to reassure him.

Dan showed him a large computer printout showing the balances for each of the clients and matters for the firm. He said the total was out of balance by about twenty thousand dollars after the conversion, so it was not an insignificant amount. He then showed them a more detailed report with a breakdown by individual client and matter. Most balances were correct as he had indicated by the check-marks beside each one. However, every fourth or fifth entry was out of balance by a few dollars which were highlighted on the report by red circles.

"Sharon and I have been going through the reports trying to figure out where the problem is," Dan said.

"Well nobody said it was going to be easy," Henry said. "Can you produce another report breaking down each balance by time and disbursements?"

"Sure," Dan said as he started hitting the keys on his keyboard.

Henry knew that law firms billed for everything. Most of an invoice would be for the lawyer's time, but they also billed for every long distance telephone call and photocopy made on behalf of a client. Henry suspected that the problem would be in the disbursements, not in the billable hours of a lawyer. The report that Dan produced a few minutes later confirmed that suspicion.

Henry started checking on the interface to their telephone system while Sharon investigated the interfaces to the firm's printers and photocopiers. Henry suggested they start their search focusing on the clients and matters that had the biggest discrepancies. It would be easier to see any patterns looking at a file that was out of balance by fifty dollars rather than one that was out by fifty cents.

It was a few hours later when Sharon found the source of the problem. The copy tracking system attached to the photocopiers on one of the floors of the firm was using an old file of valid client/matter numbers so some of their records were being rejected by the accounting system. She had found the problem by scanning log files of all of the transactions.

"I'm so sorry," Dan said when they found the source of the problem. "I thought for sure that I had converted all of those files."

"Don't worry about it," Henry said. "Anyone could have missed it. It's a lot easier to solve a problem when you have multiple people working on it."

Dan scurried to gather up all of his stuff. If he hurried, he might still be able to catch his flight.

Henry stopped by Sharon's office a few hours later as he was heading out and was surprised to see that she was still there.

"Thanks for stepping up today," Henry said, "and sorry I was missing in action this afternoon. I'm going to be counting on you to keep things running smoothly here in Chicago. I'm going to be around here for a few more days and I'd like to sit down with you to discuss how we're going to work together."

"That would be great," Sharon said, looking a little relieved. She had been worried that she would lose her job after the merger.

As Henry walked out of the office, he suddenly realized how tired he was. A lot had happened today. He didn't know that things were just getting started.

*** CHAPTER 13 ***

The next morning Henry was in the office quite early and was surprised to see Sharon already at her desk. "Good morning," Henry said. "I was going to go see Mr. McTavish this morning and give him an update on how our systems conversion is going. I was wondering if you wanted to come with me."

"Sure, if you think I can help," Sharon said. She grabbed her suit jacket from the back of her chair and slipped it on. She wasn't normally invited to meetings with the senior partner.

Henry tapped lightly on the open door when they arrived at Mr. McTavish's office. He was on the phone, but waved them in to sit at a meeting table in the corner of his office while he finished up with his call. Henry noticed that the table was covered in documents and detailed geographical maps.

"Here, let me get those out of your way," Mr. McTavish said when he got off of the phone. He quickly gathered up the documents and placed them on his desk which was already covered in paper and files.

"It looks like you're working on a large environmental litigation case," Henry said.

"No, that's actually some pro-bono work that I'm doing. I'm working with Daryl Pender from the Toronto office since it has an international element to it. What brings you two by here this morning?"

"We just wanted to give you a quick update on our systems upgrade and conversion," Henry said. "We had a bit of a hiccup yesterday but Sharon found the source of the problem so we're back on track."

"Good work Sharon," said Mr. McTavish. "We're really depending on you to make sure this all goes smoothly."

Sharon felt a little awkward receiving such praise. She was more used to lawyers complaining when things weren't going well. Henry and Sharon continued to talk as they walked back to Sharon's office. "I was going to put together a training plan for the accounting staff," Henry said, "but I think it's probably best if you take that on. You know the staff much better here in Chicago than I do."

"I think the secretaries and the paralegals will also require some additional training," Sharon said.

"You're probably right," Henry said. "We put some money in the budget for training and the only thing the partners will care about is to make sure we stay within that budget."

Sharon was more used to being told what to do and when to do it. The ability to have this much input made her feel more empowered. "I'll put together a plan and have it ready for you tomorrow."

* * *

Henry headed over to the hospital after work to see Laura. He stopped by a flower shop on the way over to pick up some flowers, but had no idea what kind of flowers that she liked. It had been quite a while since he'd bought flowers for anyone. He chose some daisies that he saw in one of the display windows because they somehow seemed more cheerful than roses.

Henry rode the elevator to the eighth floor and headed off to Laura's room. However, he was interrupted in his quest as he walked by the nurse's station. "Excuse me sir," one of the nurses called out. "Who are you here to see?"

"Laura Walsh," Henry replied. "I was here yesterday and I already know where her room is," he continued, pointing to a room that was just down the hall.

"Ms. Walsh left instructions that she didn't want to see any visitors today, except for her friend Samantha," the nurse said. Henry could see that she wasn't going to just let him stroll by and continue on to her room.

"Are you family?" asked a doctor, looking up to assess Henry. She was standing in front of the nurse's station filling in a patient's chart, but had overheard the conversation.

"No, not really," replied Henry, changing his focus to the doctor. The doctor looked like she was in her early fifties and Henry could tell she was a senior physician in the hospital, not by her age, but by the way she carried herself and the way the nurses all backed off when she had intervened. She was obviously in charge.

"So what is your relationship with Ms. Walsh?" she asked.

"Good question," Henry thought to himself - a damn good question. He suddenly realized he had no idea how to answer her. "It's sort of difficult to define," he finally blurted out.

"Try," she retorted. She wasn't going to let him off easy.

"Well, um, we sort of have a history," Henry said. "Sort of like a boyfriend, but not really. To be honest, I don't really know what our relationship is."

Henry was pretty sure she was going to ask him to leave. The nurses at the station had been listening to the conversation and looked ready to spring into action if the doctor gave the word. But she didn't. She just continued to stare at him as if she was reading his mind.

"I'm Dr. Vant," she finally said, smiling and reaching out to shake his hand. "I'm her doctor and I was just about to go see her. Come with me and we'll see if she wants to see you."

Henry walked with her toward Laura's room and struggled to keep up. Doctor's always seemed to walk with a purpose and at a quick pace. Places to go, people to see, things to do.

"Good afternoon Laura," she said as she walked into the room, pulling the curtain separating Laura's bed from the other patient as she did so. "I found this nice young man outside waiting to see you. They said you weren't taking visitors today but I thought you might want to make an exception for him. He seems pretty harmless and he's got flowers. And dear, a man who brings flowers can't be all bad."

Laura turned and looked at Henry. It was the first time she'd looked directly at him. When he'd been there yesterday, she had always kept her head down and avoided eye contact. The doctor noticed their eyes lock on each other. There was obviously something between them.

"It appears I was right," she whispered to herself. "All of your tests came back OK," the doctor said to Laura, "so I think you should be able to go home tomorrow." The doctor noticed their eyes were still locked on each other. "We'll want to do some follow-up, but I can discuss that further with you tomorrow," continued the doctor, although she wasn't sure anyone was listening. "I'll just leave you two alone now to visit."

"Thanks," Henry said, suddenly realizing he should make some kind of response.

When the doctor left the room, Laura turned on her side away from Henry and looked out the window. "I thought I asked you not to come back."

"Yeah, I guess I don't follow instructions very well," Henry said as he walked over to the other side of the bed. When he did, Laura closed her eyes. Maybe he would just take the clue and leave. He didn't.

"You know, I think you've been really brave dealing with this cancer," Henry said. "Since you caught it early, there's probably a 90% chance you'll never have to deal with it again. Samantha told me they don't think it has spread to your lymph nodes."

Henry looked at Laura. He knew she was listening, but she kept her eyes shut and didn't acknowledge him. "Some people ignore symptoms hoping they'll just go away by themselves," he said. Henry suddenly felt very emotional and it took him a few seconds to continue. "My wife couldn't deal with it and by the time she decided to go the doctor, it was too late," Henry said with a quiver in his voice.

"You're married?" Laura said, opening her eyes.

"Was," Henry said. "She passed away almost three years ago. She'd had symptoms for months and months but said she was afraid to go to the doctor. She was afraid at how I'd react. How could she even question that after all of the time we'd been together?"

Henry felt the anger and disappointment rise again that had been sitting dormant for years. "Women can be so stupid sometimes," Henry continued. "Don't they realize what's really important?"

Henry looked down at Laura and felt guilty. He was

---

making her take the fall-out from his previous relationship. Laura reached out and touched Henry's hand. "Sometimes we just forget and need to be reminded," Laura said.

Dr. Vant gave a small fist-pump and whispered "Yes" that was only audible to her. She had been secretly listening to the conversation from outside in the hallway. She had a smile a mile wide when she got back to the nurse's station and told them that Laura would be discharged the next day.

* * *

When Samantha arrived at the hospital the next day, she found Laura sitting on the edge of her bed completely dressed. However, she still continued to fuss as she put on a big bulky sweater, then took it off, and then put it back on again. The nurse had confirmed that morning that she would be discharged today but she was still waiting for the doctor to arrive to give her any final instructions about the next steps.

"Sorry I'm late," Samantha said when she walked in the room.

"You're not," Laura replied. "I'm still waiting for the doctor to arrive. The nurse said they really had no idea when the doctor would get here, but thought it could be anytime between 11AM and 3PM." It was already almost 1PM and Laura was growing more and more impatient.

"How do I look?" Laura asked. "I mean, can you tell…?"

She didn't finish the question, but Samantha knew what she was asking. "You look just fine," Samantha said, trying to reassure her.

"Do you have anything to take the flowers in?" Laura asked.

"Flowers?" Samantha asked, raising an eyebrow. She was pretty sure she knew who had brought Laura the flowers, but waited to see how Laura would respond.

"Henry brought them yesterday," Laura said, feeling her face starting to blush. "The nurse loaned me a vase to put them in but she wants the vase back when I leave. I want to take them with me and I don't want them to die."

"Good afternoon ladies," said Dr. Vant when she came walking into the room. "You get to go home today, but I'd like to talk to you about where we go from here. As you know, the surgery went very well and our tests indicated that it hasn't spread to your lymph nodes. However, we recommend that we follow up with a few sessions of radiation."

"Is that really necessary?" Laura asked.

"It's not mandatory, but I'd highly recommend it," the doctor said. "It's just precautionary. Even though our tests indicated the cancer has not spread, we'd like you to have fifteen radiation treatments just to be sure. If it's OK with you, we'd like to start those treatments in about ten days."

"Sure," Laura replied, although she still seemed a little apprehensive.

"Is this your ride home?" the doctor asked, smiling at Samantha.

"Yes," Samantha replied. "And I'll be staying with her for a while to keep an eye on her."

Samantha had originally invited Laura to stay at her place while she recuperated, but Laura had insisted she wanted to go home to her own place. It made more sense anyway as Samantha's apartment was a small one-bedroom apartment whereas Laura had purchased a two-bedroom condo a few years ago. However, Samantha had insisted she move into Laura's extra bedroom for a few weeks so she could take care of her until she was fully back on her feet.

They had just settled into a taxi outside of the hospital when Samantha's cell phone rang. She fumbled to get it out of her purse and smiled when she saw who was calling. "Hi Henry," she said, smiling at Laura when she said it.

"Yes, she was just discharged," she continued. "We're on our way back to Laura's place right now. Do you want to talk to her?"

"He wants to talk to you," Samantha said as she handed the phone to Laura.

Laura took the phone from Samantha and half-turned her shoulder away from her, as if by doing so her conversation would somehow be more private. She continued to play with the petals of the daisies that sat on her lap as she spoke. The nurse had been nice enough to wrap them up so they remained protected during the trip home.

"Yes…..OK…..That's not really necessary…..Sure, if you want to……OK……Bye," Laura said. It was obvious that Henry was doing most of the talking. She handed the phone back to Samantha.

"Well?" Samantha asked, her eyes widening with excitement. "What's happening?"

Laura looked away and out her side of the taxi as it made its way to her condo. "He's heading back to Toronto tonight," Laura said. "He said he'll be back in Chicago the week after next and asked if he could pop over to see how I'm doing."

"And?" Samantha asked.

"I said it wasn't really necessary, but he could if he wanted to."

"He's good for you, you know," Samantha said. "And it's probably a bit late to be playing hard-to-get."

Laura couldn't hide the smile on her face as the taxi pulled up in front of her condo building.

"We're home," she said.

*** CHAPTER 14 ***

Henry felt exhausted as he flew from Chicago back to Toronto. It had been a long week. But it had been a good week, all things considered. He'd managed to get the software upgrades completed at the firm and the partners seemed happy. But more importantly, he'd finally found out who the secret woman from the airport was and connected with her again.

When he got back home later that evening, he headed for the La-Z-Boy chair, turned on the TV and reclined his chair to the full-back position. He didn't know what was on the TV schedule for that night, and didn't really care, but flipped from one channel to the next using the remote control. He was pleased when he heard David coming through the back door.

"Hi Dad," he said as he came into the living room and slumped on the couch. "What-cha watching?"

"Nothing really," Henry said. "I just turned it on. So how's your week been?"

"OK," David replied mindlessly. "Oh, I almost forgot," he said, suddenly perking up. "I heard from the U-19 coaches. They want me to come to a training session at the indoor field up in Vaughan next Saturday. Alex was asked to go as well. I'm really excited about it, but also a little scared."

"You'll do fine," Henry said. "They wouldn't have asked you to attend if they didn't think you were up for it."

"How was your week in Chicago?" David asked.

Henry told him about the software upgrades they'd completed, but he could tell David wasn't really interested. He didn't tell him about Laura. He wasn't quite ready to start telling the family about her just yet.

Henry continued to channel surf, but stopped when he reached the local news station. He hadn't been keeping up with any of the local news while he was away in Chicago. Henry heard the first couple of stories, but was gradually drifting off to sleep.

"You know, I think our political system is completely broken," David said, pulling Henry back from his semi-conscious state.

Henry hadn't been following the last few minutes of the newscast, but one of the stories had obviously triggered the statement from David. "I'm sure there are a lot of people who would agree with you," Henry said. "What made you come to that realization now?"

"Well, the first story was about a new initiative that the federal Conservatives announced and the Liberals immediately came out against it," David said. "The next story was about what the provincial Liberals are doing and both the NDP and Conservatives are against it. It's like they're immediately against whatever the other party is for, regardless of what it is."

"That's politics," Henry said. "It's worse in the US. The Democrats and Republicans would rather do something to hurt the other party than to do something that would help the country." Henry had seen the same useless bickering going on when he was in Chicago. "Both parties threatened to let the U.S. fall off the fiscal cliff rather than compromise and come up with a budget that both parties could live with."

"Yeah, but it's like they set up the whole political system to fail," David continued. "I mean, they call the other party, whoever they are, the opposition. By definition, they oppose everything the government tries to do. I think they'd be better off getting rid of all of the parties, just let all of them be independent. That way, each person would be accountable for their own actions and not just vote for something because their party told them to."

"I think you've got a point," Henry said. "Maybe when you're older, you can do something to change it."

"I'm not sure we can wait that long - It's just so frustrating!" David said as he walked out of the living room. "Good night," he said as he walked down the hall toward his bedroom.

"Good night, David." It had been a while since Henry had thought about politics and realized how apathetic he'd become. He was glad the youth of the world challenged the way things were done. That was the only hope that things would eventually change.

He switched his focus back to the TV but could feel himself drifting off to sleep again. The last thing he remembered hearing was about a snow storm that would be arriving later in the week.

* * *

The weather forecasters had been right. The first real snow storm of the year had arrived on Friday, although it wasn't as big as they had predicted. It was mostly centred around the Great Lakes, called a lake-effect snow storm.

Alan was making his way to the Toronto Island Airport and was glad that he had chosen to take public transit. The first snow storm of the season always seemed to trigger a lot of fender-benders. People seemed to forget how to drive in snow from one year to the next.

Alan only had to wait a minute or two for the next ferry to arrive to take him over to the island. When he got to the other side, he saw Edward Bronson waiting for him. Edward was a licensed pilot and had his own small plane that he kept at the airport. He was a high flying executive in more ways than one. He normally flew on one of the commercial airlines or used one of his companies' corporate jets, but this was a flight he wanted to handle himself.

"Are you sure you want to fly in this weather?" Alan asked as he approached.

"It shouldn't be a problem, provided I get in the air before it gets any worse," Edward said. "The snow squalls disappear once you get about twenty-five miles from here."

"I brought the suit," Alan said, showing him the suit he had slung over his arm. Alan walked with him as he headed out to his plane which had already been fueled and was ready to go. "I've always wanted to go to New York, but never had the opportunity," Alan said. "How long does it take to get there?"

"I should be in New York in no time at all. However, getting back tomorrow might be a different story if this weather persists. If you've got your passport with you, you can come along if you want."

Alan reached inside the zippered pocket of his jacket and was pleased to see that his passport was there. He normally didn't carry his passport, but had used it earlier that week to attend a Sabres hockey game in Buffalo and hadn't bothered to take it out. Alan was excited by the thought of flying into New York on a private plane as he'd always wanted to live like the rich and famous. He didn't have to work the next day, so that wouldn't be a problem.

"I have my passport with me, but I don't have any place to stay," Alan said.

"I'm sure we can find some accommodations for you," Edward said. "That won't be a problem - my treat."

They climbed into the aircraft and Alan was immediately impressed. This was no rinky-dink plane as it had all of the latest technology. Although the visibility was limited by the snow squalls, Edward was fully qualified to fly by instruments only. He had done it hundreds of times before.

As they taxied out onto the runway, Alan noticed a dark blue car parked by the fence. When a snow plow went by, the blue beacon light on the top of the plow showed the shadows of two men who were sitting in the car. He thought they might be security or customs agents watching for anyone arriving or departing that wasn't supposed to. But he was flying with Edward Bronson, one of the most important men in Canada, so he felt confident they wouldn't be questioning them about this trip. Mr. Bronson flew to New York all of the time.

After the plane took off, one of the men in the car flipped open his cell phone and hit the buttons to call one of his contacts. "It's Carter. Bronson's plane just took off. Everything has been taken care of."

He flipped off his phone and turned to his partner. "OK, let's go," he said. The lights on the dark blue car lit up and it turned out through a gate at the airport and into the night. Their work for the evening had been completed.

Up in the air, Alan felt quite nervous. He couldn't see anything but snow and darkness looking out of the windows. Edward sensed his nervousness. "The key is to focus on the instruments," he said. He explained each of the instruments as he pointed to them, the attitude indicator or artificial horizon, the vertical speed indicator, the altimeter, and the gyro. Alan didn't understand anything that Edward was saying but he was right - he felt more at ease focusing on the instruments than he did by looking out of the window.

Alan's heart skipped a beat when the instrument panel suddenly flickered and went dark, but everything lit up again a second later.

"That was weird," Edward said. "I'll have to get them to look at that after we land."

They continued on their flight to New York. Edward could sense that Alan was still a bit nervous about flying so he changed the conversation to help take his mind off it. "I'm quite pleased at the progress that we're making on the environmental project," Edward said. "The environmentalists came up with a pretty good approach to the new pipeline. They re-routed the pipeline to avoid most of the geographic areas of concern and where they couldn't, they proposed using extra sensors and controls every five hundred metres. That way, if there's ever a leak, they can automatically shut off the flow of oil at the last control within seconds. In less environmentally sensitive areas, the controls are only every few kilometres."

"Do you think the oil companies will agree to the extra cost?" Alan asked.

"The cost will be a lot less than the billions of dollars it would cost them to clean up the mess without those sensors. I've had a couple of lawyers put the whole plan together along with a budget. That's what's in the package that you've nested inside my suit. The courier in New York will be delivering that package to a few different companies to see if they will buy into the solution."

"What if they don't?" Alan asked.

"I always have a backup plan," Edward said. "That

package is also being delivered to some companies on the west coast along with a few key people in Washington. In the end, I think we'll get it right but we can't let one or two people sidetrack the whole solution. Always have a backup plan."

Alan felt pleased that he had set up his own backup plan. Since his latest bipolar episode, he had come to realize how important it was. Alan checked his watch and noticed that they had now been in the air for almost half an hour but they were obviously still in the snow squalls. "I thought you said we'd be out of the snow squalls by now."

"We should have been," Edward replied. "The storm must have moved further south than what they indicated in the forecast they gave me before we took off."

Edward sensed Alan's nervousness, so tried to change his focus again. "I've also just started a new project, one to tackle gun control. I've already got a few people lined up to tackle the problem because it's an issue that should have been addressed years ago. I'm optimistic we'll be able to come up with something."

Suddenly there was another flicker of the instrument panel and all of the dials went dark. This time they didn't come back on. To make matters worse, there was a distinct odour of something burning. Alan was now in full panic mode. But Edward maintained his calmness and reached beneath his seat and pulled out a flashlight and shone it on the instrument panel. They showed nothing. He then shone the flashlight underneath the dashboard and started pulling at the wires to see if he could see where the short was.

"What the hell?" Edward said. He could see that they had been tampered with as several of the wires had been stripped and others had burned through their casings. "We've lost our instruments, but the plane seems to be flying OK. If we keep flying in the same direction, we should be out of the storm shortly and then I'll be able to fly by sight again. We'll be OK. Remember, I always have a backup plan."

It was hard to determine if Edward was saying that to calm Alan down, or to reassure himself. He tried the radio, but it was dead as well. They both stared out of the plane into the snow and the darkness. It was like they were staring into the abyss.

*** CHAPTER 15 ***

David was overly excited on Saturday morning as he got ready for his first training session with the Under-19 team. It was still a little before 8AM but he had been lying in bed awake for at least the last hour and a half. He decided he should just probably get up and start getting ready.

"Hi Dad," he said as he walked into the kitchen.

"All ready for your big day?" Henry asked. Henry was excited about David's first training session as well. "Have you got everything you're supposed to bring today?"

"Oh shit," David replied. "Everyone is supposed to bring their own soccer ball but I forgot to ask the coach to loan me one of the team's balls. Mine is pretty beat up from kicking it around on the driveway." David hesitated before he spoke again, as if trying to anticipate the answer before he asked the question. "Do you think Uncle Alan would mind if I used the soccer ball he got me for my birthday at the tryout?"

"I think he'd be thrilled," Henry replied. "I think he'd rather see you use it than just keeping it in a box on your shelf."

David went to his bedroom and pulled the soccer ball down from the shelf that held all of the various soccer trophies he'd won since he was little. When he pulled it from the box, he could see that it was actually a high quality leather ball. If only it had the Adidas logo rather than the Goliath logo. Oh well, he'd just tell the others it was just a practice ball if anyone asked.

Henry and David headed out of the house about half an hour later to start the drive to the soccer dome in Vaughan. There shouldn't be as much traffic on a Saturday so Henry didn't think it would take them that long to get there. As he headed out the door, Henry grabbed the newspaper that had been shoved into his mailbox. It would be nice to have something to read if the practice got too boring.

When they got to the soccer dome, David went to the registration table to check in and he was given a binder and told which part of the field he should report to. The field was divided into four sections and it seemed like there were more coaches and trainers than there were players.

Henry climbed into the small seating section with all of the other parents to watch the proceedings. In one part of the field, the players were being timed by the coaches as they ran what looked like about a 40 yard dash, first forwards and then backwards. In another part of the field, players were doing long jumps and jumping over small hurdles from a standing start, again with coaches measuring everything.

The third section, which is where David had been sent, was the only section where they were actually using a soccer ball as the players dribbled a ball around pylons. Henry watched closely when it was David's turn to run through the drill. He thought he was one of the fastest he had seen do the drill, until he lost control of the ball while going around one of the pylons and almost fell. Henry was sure that David's nervousness accounted for the mistake. The coach that was working that section patted David on the shoulder and told him to try it again. This time David completed the drill without making any mistakes, but he was noticeably slower than the first time he'd tried it.

The fourth section had players being weighed and measured, others doing sit-ups and push-ups, and others riding stationary bikes wearing all kinds of contraptions that Henry assumed were measuring heart rate and lung capacity. This wasn't what Henry was expecting at all. This wasn't just a bunch of kids kicking a soccer ball around the field with some coaches watching the proceedings. Everything seemed to be being measured and quantified.

After about 20 minutes, someone blew a whistle and the players moved to the next station. Henry watched as David completed the various activities. He had no idea how David was doing in comparison with the other kids. When David got to the section measuring speed, he could see that David was one of the best. There were a few who could match David's speed running forward, but many almost stumbled when they tried to run backwards.

When they had completed each of the sections, the coaches gathered all of the kids together and seemed to be explaining the next steps, but Henry couldn't really hear what they were saying. Henry was sure the coaches had deliberately gathered the players together on the far side of the field so the parents couldn't hear. In too many cases, the parents considered themselves coaches as well.

The kids had now been out there over two hours and Henry was sure they were tired. He knew he was, and he had just been watching the proceedings. Since he couldn't hear the coaches anyway, Henry pulled out the newspaper that he had brought with him to see what was going on in the world. There was the usual picture of some celebrity doing something embarrassing but it was the headline near the bottom right of the front page that caught Henry's eye.

"Edward Bronson Plane Missing," read the headline.

The story explained that Edward Bronson's plane had taken off from the Toronto Island airport the night before on a planned trip to New York, but it had never arrived. There had been no reports of a crash and there was now a search underway along the planned route to try to find any signs of the plane. So far, nothing had been found but the search was continuing. The article indicated that Mr. Bronson had taken off in a snow storm but was an experienced pilot and had flown in such weather before.

Henry had just finished reading the article when he saw David and Alex walking off the field toward the stands where he was sitting. Henry knew that Alex was also supposed to be at these tryouts as well, but hadn't really noticed him out on the field.

"How did it go out there guys?" Henry asked as they got closer.

"I'm exhausted," David replied. "Dad, can we give Alex a ride home? His mom had to leave to head to another appointment, but I thought we'd be able to give him a ride."

"No problem," Henry said, gathering up his things.

On the drive home, David explained that the coaches would be back for another session in five or six weeks. "They're running similar training camps in the Maritimes, Quebec, Alberta and British Columbia which is why there are the big gaps in time. In the meantime, we're supposed to follow the individual instructions that they gave us. The players for the team will be picked for a few "Friendlies" to be held over the next several months." Henry knew that "Friendlies" was the term that soccer teams used to describe exhibition games that weren't part of a competition like the World Cup, but he also knew that these games were extremely important to the players on the teams.

David and Alex locked into their own conversation as they compared each of their results that were recorded in their binders. Henry was only catching portions of their conversation.

"What was your time going through the pylons?....Yeah, I sucked at that one....I thought I was going to puke after doing the sit-ups," went the conversation back and forth.

"Dad, there are about a million release forms you'll have to sign," David said, bringing Henry back into the conversation. "And they want both Alex and I to work with a trainer to put on some weight. I think they pay for everything."

"I doubt that," Henry said.

"Yeah, I'm not really sure," David said. "It's all in the binder. You can look at it later."

Henry looked in the rear view mirror and noticed that both David and Alex had now slumped into their seats. Their excitement had now been replaced by exhaustion.

*** CHAPTER 16 ***

On Monday morning, Henry headed off on a two-day trip to the Chicago office. Things were actually running quite smoothly in Chicago since the merger was finalized.

Henry was also looking forward to seeing Laura again. He had arranged to head over to her place for dinner that evening. Samantha would be there as well as she was still staying at Laura's condo to help out until Laura was fully recovered. Henry had offered to take them both out for dinner, but Laura said she wasn't ready for a night out on the town just yet. Henry stopped at the flower shop and picked up some more daisies on his way over.

Laura's condo was on the north side of Chicago and she had suggested that he take the train because her condo was fairly close to the Clark/Division stop, but Henry had decided to take a taxi because he didn't really understand the color-coded system used in Chicago and was afraid he'd get on the wrong train or miss the stop. That turned out to be a mistake because they had encountered an accident on the way and the taxi driver had to navigate his way through the back streets to get around it. Henry checked his watch as he buzzed Laura's suite and realized he was about twenty minutes late. He hated being late for anything.

"Hi, it's Henry," he said into the speaker when she answered. "Sorry I'm late."

"No problem," Laura said. "Come on up, tenth floor."

Henry felt surprisingly nervous as he rode up the elevator. He put on his best smile as he knocked on her door, but it was actually Samantha who opened the door.

"Hi Henry," Samantha said. "Come on in. Laura's just finishing preparing dinner."

Henry apologized again for being late as he stepped in. Laura's condo was much larger than he expected, or at least appeared much larger than it really was. The living room, dining room and kitchen were all really just one room, with an island with four stools separating the living room from the kitchen, and a big green plant separating the living room from the dining room. The window in the living room was enormous and included patio doors that led out onto a narrow balcony. Although Laura's condo was several blocks from the lake, you could clearly see Lake Michigan as the surrounding buildings didn't obstruct her view.

"Nice view," Henry said.

"It was one of the main reasons why I purchased this place," Laura said from the kitchen.

Henry continued to scan the condo. Everything seemed so clean, with a white leather sofa and chair, glass and silver end tables and beige, almost-white carpet. Henry quickly checked his shoes to make sure he hadn't tracked in any dirt.

The whole room looked like the cover photo of a Modern Homes and Gardens magazine, with one exception. At the far end of the room sat a large glass and silver desk with a white leather chair. That fit the profile of the room, but the desk was covered in what looked like a year's worth of newspapers, magazines and books. There were more than could fit on the desk as evidenced by a pile of newspapers that had obviously slid off the back of the desk onto the floor.

"I'd just like to point out that I'm making no promises about my cooking," Laura said as she placed the meal on the dining room table. "It's only spaghetti, but I'm worried that I may have over-cooked it."

"My favourite," Henry said as he approached Laura and tried to give her a hug. Laura pulled her sweater around her and held her hands in front of her as Henry hugged her and gave her a quick kiss on the cheek. It was obvious Laura was still very self-conscious about how she looked.

"Let me get you a vase for those," Laura said as she pulled away. Henry was oblivious to the fact that he had been walking around carrying the flowers since he'd arrived. Laura quickly returned with a vase and placed the flowers in the centre of the table.

"This is my contribution," Samantha said as she pulled some garlic bread from the oven and placed it in a basket on one side of the table. "I bought it myself," she said grinning.

"Everything looks delicious," Henry said as he sat down.

As they ate, they continued to make small talk about the view from Laura's condo and how good the meal was. It was apparent they were running out of things to talk about and they knew they'd hit rock bottom when they started talking about the weather. After an incredibly long pause in the conversation, Samantha broke the silence. "So Henry, Laura tells me you were married before. How long were you married? Do you have any kids?"

Laura looked at Samantha with amazement as to how she could be so intrusive.

"Don't look at me like that," Samantha said. "You know

you want to know as much as I do."

"So spill the details," Samantha said, turning her focus back to Henry.

Henry put his knife and fork down and smiled. "We were married almost eighteen years. Mindy and I met in our first year at university and got married in our second year. She dropped out in third year when she got pregnant with our first son, Robert, who's now almost twenty. Our second son, David, just turned eighteen. Both boys live with me in a suburb west of Toronto. Mindy passed away almost three years ago but my mother also lives with us part of the year, which is a real help. She spends about five months a year down in Florida and spends the rest of the year either living with us, or with my older sister, Jenny. I also have a younger brother, Alan. My dad passed away about twelve years ago."

"And you work for a law firm?" Samantha asked.

"Gawd!" groaned Laura. "Give the guy a break. She won't stop until she's got your medical history and your last three tax returns," continued Laura, giving Henry a look of sympathy.

"Yes, I work for a law firm, but I'm not a lawyer," Henry said. "I'm the Information Technology Director. We just merged with a Chicago firm which is why I'm here every few weeks."

"So do you both work for the Tribune?" Henry asked, turning the conversation in the other direction.

"Yes we do," Samantha replied. "I work in the Lifestyles department - you know things like Health, Travel and Fine Dining. But Laura has a very interesting job. She's an investigative journalist. Why don't you tell him more about your job, Laura?"

"I'm not sure I want to play this truth or consequences game you've started," Laura replied. "Besides, I have to clear the table," she said as she rose and started carrying stuff into the kitchen. She grabbed Samantha's plate out from under her, even though she was clearly not finished.

"The meal was delicious," Henry said, picking up his own plate to carry into the kitchen.

"You don't have to clear," Laura said. "You and Samantha can retire to the living room. I'm sure she wants to continue with your interrogation."

Laura continued to clear the table while Henry and Samantha went to sit on the white leather couch in the living room. When Laura looked in a few minutes later, she noticed that Samantha was now showing Henry pictures from one of her photo albums. "What are you into now?" Laura asked as she headed into the living room and sat on the leather chair.

"Well, if you're not going to tell him all about yourself, I thought I'd give him your life history in pictures," Samantha said, teasing Laura.

"Just kill me now, please," Laura said, obviously embarrassed.

"This is her mom and dad," continued Samantha pointing out the people in the pictures. She continued turning pages of the album, explaining them as she went. "Oh, this is a good one," continued Samantha. "This is when she was crowned the prom queen at her high school. How old were you in this picture Laura, seventeen or so?"

"OK, that's enough of that," Laura said, grabbing the photo album from Samantha. But Henry had already seen the photo. He'd also seen the date on the photo and doing quick calculations in his head, had determined that Laura was probably only thirty-four or so, nine years younger than he was. He suddenly felt quite old.

"All right," Samantha said. "But at least show him the photo of the group of us from work."

Laura flipped several more pages of the album and then came and sat with them on the couch. "This is obviously me and Sam," Laura said pointing at the picture. She then rhymed off the names of the others in the picture.

"They've all been asking when you're coming back to work," Samantha said. "They ask all of the time how you're doing."

"I'm not ready yet," Laura said. "Don't forget, I start my radiation treatments next week. I need more time before I head back to work."

"That reminds me," Samantha said. "I have to go out of town next Wednesday and Thursday so I won't be able to be here to help you out if you need it. Henry, any chance you could be here on those days to check up on her?"

"Absolutely," Henry said. "Just tell me what you need."

"Don't I get a vote in this?" interjected Laura.

"Yes you do," Samantha replied. "But so do Henry and I, and we can out-vote you two to one. Besides, if you don't agree to let Henry help you out, I'm going to cancel my trip and it will be your fault if they fire me."

"I'm sure I'll be fine by myself," Laura replied, but she already knew she wasn't going to win this argument.

"Settled," Samantha said. "You can stay in the second bedroom. I'll just move my stuff out of the way for a few days." Samantha looked quite proud of herself for orchestrating this solution. She excused herself on the pretext of needing something from the bedroom, but it was obvious she just wanted to leave Henry and Laura alone.

"Don't let her bully you into feeling like you have to be here next week," Laura said after Samantha was out of ear-shot. "I'm sure I'll be just fine."

"I'm sure you will, but it's always nice to have someone around just in case. The actual radiation treatments are no big deal, just like going in for an X-ray. You won't feel a thing."

Laura assumed that Henry knew about radiation treatments because of his wife's ordeal several years ago. She wanted to ask him more questions, but didn't want to impose.

"It varies from patient to patient and the areas they're planning to zap, but you might feel a little queasy a few hours after your treatment," Henry continued. "But it usually goes away after a few hours. Have they drawn the targets on you yet?"

Laura pulled her sweater around her and hugged herself tightly. It was obvious by her reaction that they had. In fact, it had been done earlier that day at the hospital. They had weighed and measured her precisely and had drawn lines on her chest which would be used to align the equipment so they could make sure the radiation precisely hit the areas they wanted. Laura had looked at herself in the mirror when she got home and felt like the poster she'd seen at the grocery store which showed where the various cuts of beef come from. She desperately wanted to wash all of the markings off but they had told her to leave them there until all of her treatments were completed.

Henry had wanted to make Laura feel more at ease about her upcoming radiation treatments, but he was now worried that maybe he was having the opposite effect. It was hard to know how much information anyone needed or wanted. Sometimes not knowing was worse than the actual event, but other times it seemed like a person is better off not knowing what lay ahead for them. Henry sensed that Laura had now reached her threshold, at least for now.

"I should probably get going," Henry said, glancing at his watch and rising from the couch. Laura followed him to the door.

"Thanks again for supper," he said as he slipped on his

coat. Henry reached out to give Laura a hug and kissed her on the forehead as he pulled her in close. She continued to hug herself, but liked how Henry's arms felt around her. She somehow felt more protected from anything bad that lay in her future when Henry held her.

"You'll be fine, trust me," Henry said, trying to reassure her. "I'll be back next Tuesday. Don't hesitate to call me if you need anything in the meantime."

Laura lingered in his embrace a little longer, but then seemed to will herself to be strong again. After Henry left, Laura watched him through the peep-hole as he walked down the hallway towards the elevators. She continued to watch until he got on the elevator. She was glad that Henry would be coming back again.

*** CHAPTER 17 ***

On Wednesday morning, Henry sat at the kitchen table reading the newspaper as he ate breakfast. There was still a headline on the front page about Edward Bronson's plane being missing, but there were only a few lines of text before referring the reader to an inner page for more details. That's because they really didn't have anything more to report. They had expanded their search area but had not found anything yet. Henry folded the paper under his arm as he headed for the door. He would read the rest of the paper on the train as it headed into Toronto. When Henry opened the front door, he was surprised to see a strange car in the driveway and two people walking up his front steps.

"Good morning sir," said the first man. "Are you Henry Shaw?"

"Yes," Henry replied, looking confused.

"Are you the brother of Alan Shaw?" said the stranger, continuing his questioning.

"Yes," Henry replied. "What's this about?"

"I'm Detective Benedetti and this is Detective Fleming," he replied, as both of the strangers pulled identification out of their pockets and showed it to Henry. "Could we step inside to explain?"

Henry nervously invited both of them into the living room, fearing what they were going to say next. "Are you aware of Edward Bronson's plane having gone missing?" Detective Benedetti asked.

"Yes, I was just reading about it in this morning's paper," Henry replied, pulling the newspaper out from under his arm.

"We have reason to believe your brother may have been on that plane. Have you spoken to your brother in the last few days?"

"No, I've been out of town," replied Henry, trying to remember the last time he'd spoken to Alan. "I tried calling him last weekend, but I just got his voice-mail, but that's not out of the ordinary." Henry pulled his cell phone from his pocket and pressed the keys to select Alan from his list of contacts, desperately hoping that Alan would answer and this would all to be proven to be a mistake, but the call went directly to his voice-mail.

"Do you know if your brother was an acquaintance of Mr. Bronson?" Detective Benedetti asked. Henry noticed that the other detective had taken out a notebook and was taking notes on everything that Henry said.

"My brother works at a menswear store in Toronto and I know that he sold some suits to Mr. Bronson," Henry said, recalling the day he'd seen him at the store several weeks ago. "But I didn't think he really knew him personally, at least not well enough to be flying with him on his plane. What makes you think Alan was on the plane?"

"We reviewed video from the airport the night Mr. Bronson's plane went missing and your brother was seen talking to Mr. Bronson. We don't know if your brother got on the plane with him or not, but the footage shows them heading out toward the plane together. Could you let us know immediately if you hear anything from your brother?" The detective pulled a card from his pocket and handed it to Henry.

"Certainly," Henry replied.

"There must be some mistake," said a voice from the hallway. Henry turned to see his mother standing there looking as white as a ghost. She had been listening to the whole conversation. "Alan wouldn't have gotten on that plane. He was afraid to fly." Her voice started to crack as she said the last few words.

"This is our mother," Henry said, explaining her presence to the detectives.

"I'm sure you're right," Detective Benedetti said, trying to reassure her. "But we have to follow up on all possible leads. We're sorry to have troubled you."

"Please call me if you hear anything," the detective said, turning his focus back to Henry.

Henry watched as the officers headed to their car and drove off. He then turned to his mother and gave her a reassuring hug. "I'm sure it's all a mistake," he said.

Henry told his mother he was heading off to work, trying to give the impression that this was just a minor hiccup in a normal day. He must have called Alan's number twenty times on the train ride into Toronto, but they all went immediately to voice-mail. Alan's mailbox was now full so he couldn't even leave another message for him.

When he got to Toronto, he didn't head into work, but headed immediately to the menswear store hoping he would see Alan measuring someone up for a new suit. But he didn't. His co-workers said they hadn't seen him for a few days and he had already missed several of his scheduled shifts.

Henry then headed off to Alan's apartment. He

convinced Manuel, the superintendent, to let him into Alan's apartment. Maybe Alan had gone off his medications again and he would be found sleeping in his apartment. But he wasn't. Manuel said he couldn't remember the last time he'd seen Alan, but he thought it was at least a week ago.

Henry called Jenny next. "Have you heard anything from Alan in the last few days?"

"No," Jenny replied. "Why, what's the matter?"

Henry explained the visit he had received that morning from the police. He told her that he'd already been to Alan's work and his apartment and there was no sign of him at either place.

"I know he was supposed to go to a hockey game in Buffalo last week with some old friends from high school," Jenny said. "Maybe he's off on some bender with them."

"Do you know which friends?"

"I know Marty was one of them and Stoney was the guy who got the tickets. I don't know their last names. Do you remember them from high school?" Henry didn't know Marty's last name either but he knew "Stoney" was the nickname for Terry Stonefield, as Henry had gone to school with his older brother. Henry found a telephone number for him on the internet and he confirmed that they'd all gone to the hockey game and come back together on a shuttle-bus. He hadn't seen or spoken to Alan since that night.

No one knew where Alan was. Henry feared the worse.

* * *

On the following Tuesday morning, Henry picked up a newspaper at the small store in the airport while he was waiting for his flight to Chicago. He had already read his regular paper at home that morning, but he picked up a different one hoping it might have some additional news about Edward Bronson and his brother that wasn't in the first paper. He had been checking the newspaper every morning and Detective Benedetti had called him that morning to give him an update.

"We don't have anything more to report," Detective Benedetti said, "but I thought I'd give you a heads-up that we released your brother's name to the press." In the first reports about the loss of the plane, it had only mentioned Edward Bronson's name. Then a few days later it said Mr. Bronson and an associate were missing, but they didn't name the associate. The detective explained that releasing Alan's name wasn't to give the newshounds something more to nibble on, but he was hoping that someone would come forward with additional information about his brother. "We still don't have any confirmation that Alan was ever on that plane with Mr. Bronson and I hope we're wrong, but it becomes more and more likely with each passing day without any sign of either of them."

Even though he had been warned that it was coming, it was still hard to read Alan's name in the paper. It made it harder to believe that this was just going to turn out to be some kind of mistake. His mother refused to read the articles in the paper, perhaps pretending that if she didn't read it that it would mean that it hadn't really happened.

Henry hated leaving his mother at this time and Jenny had agreed to stay with her while he was out of town. In some ways, Henry was glad to be getting away to Chicago. Of course, he was looking forward to seeing Laura but it also gave him the opportunity to put his worries about Alan on hold for a while.

The partners at the firm had told Henry that he could have cancelled his trip to Chicago and stayed closer to home until his brother's situation was resolved. But Henry had told them he thought it was best to try to continue with some kind of normal work routine. He hadn't told them about his other interest in going to Chicago.

When Henry got to Chicago, he spent most of the day doing "busy-work", things like approving timesheets and invoices. He had trouble keeping his focus. Midway through the day he tried calling Laura to see how she was doing, but he didn't get an answer. Henry knew that Laura would have had her first radiation treatment the day before. He decided to call Samantha.

"Hi Samantha," he said when she answered. "It's Henry. Sorry to bug you during your work day but I was wondering how Laura did yesterday. I tried calling her myself, but didn't get an answer."

"The radiation treatment went really well," Samantha answered. "She had her treatment about 4PM and came out beaming that it was no big deal at all. But then she started feeling bad after supper and spent the night throwing up. I felt guilty leaving her this morning, but she seemed to be sleeping soundly when I left the condo."

"She shouldn't have eaten supper," Henry said.

"Yeah, they had suggested that at the hospital but Laura said she felt great and was starving. Big mistake, I guess. You're still going to be there tonight, right? I'm leaving shortly for Denver for my work project but I'll be back on Thursday."

"Yeah, I'll be heading over to her place after work today," Henry said.

"Thanks so much. I've got to run. I can see them standing at the elevators waiting for me. Take care." The line went dead before Henry had a chance to say anything more.

When Henry arrived at Laura's condo after work, he was pleased to see her looking good when she opened the door.

She noticed the bag of groceries he was carrying. "You didn't have to bring groceries. I'm not completely helpless you know. I've got enough food in the house so we don't starve over the next few days."

"Yeah, but do you have these?" Henry asked as he pulled what looked like the world's biggest box of Rice Krispies from the shopping bag.

"Let me guess," she said. "This has been your favourite cereal since you were a kid and you won't start your day without them. Whatever turns your crank."

"Actually, they're for you. Samantha told me you had a rough night last night and I think you'll find these will help."

"That was my own fault," Laura said. "They told me at the hospital to watch what I eat after the treatment, but I felt fine so I thought I'd be able to share a pizza with Samantha. Not one of my smartest moves. I'm going to skip supper tonight altogether but there's plenty of food here so you can make something for yourself."

"You'll have to eat something later on tonight or else you'll just get run down. You can't give up eating completely for the next three weeks."

Sure enough, Laura said she was feeling a little green around the gills about 7PM and headed off to her bedroom to lie down. Henry plopped himself down on the couch and watched a Blackhawks game that was on TV. Laura emerged from her bedroom about 11PM, but still looked a little queasy.

"How are you feeling?" Henry asked.

"A little better," Laura replied.

"Care to join me for a bowl of Rice Krispies?" Henry asked as he opened a few cupboard doors until he found the bowls.

"Are you sure this is a good idea? I'm not sure I'm really

up to eating anything yet."

"Trust me," Henry said, as he poured cereal into both bowls. "I think you'll find this will settle your stomach for the night." Laura took a few mouthfuls and was surprised that she started feeling better almost immediately. She poured herself another bowl when she finished the first.

"So, it seems I told you my life's story the other night but you carefully avoided divulging anything," Henry said.

"You noticed that, did you?" Laura said. "I'd like to tell you more, but I think I'm feeling a little queasy again." Laura flashed a sly smile.

"Nice try," Henry said.

"So what would you like to know?" Laura asked, a little apprehensively.

"Anything," Henry said. "Well, everything actually - but let's start with relationships."

"I've never been married," Laura said. "I lived with a guy for almost six years. It was great for both of us while we were together. We were both focused on our careers at the time. I don't know why I was surprised when he proposed, but I told him I needed some more time to decide. I couldn't think of a single reason why I shouldn't marry him, but I never did say yes. He eventually grew tired of waiting."

Laura seemed lost in thought for a moment as if reliving the day that she had come home to find that Todd had left. "I've had a couple of brief relationships since then, but nothing serious," Laura continued. "I'm an only child. My mom died in a car accident when I was twelve. My dad is still alive and remarried almost ten years ago, but I never really hit it off with his new wife so we've gradually drifted apart. Samantha's my best friend and has been since we were little."

"So what do you do for fun?" Henry asked.

"You mean, besides picking up guys in airport bars?" Laura replied. "Actually, I don't do much other than work, or at least up until now. Work was my whole life and now I'm not even sure if I want to go back."

Laura paused again as if searching her mind trying to figure out who she was or who'd she become. "You must have thought I was a real slut when I approached you at that bar," Laura said. "I'm not really like that. I'm not sure who that person was. It was almost like someone else had taken control of me and I was just going along for the ride."

"At first I thought you were a hooker," Henry said. "My logic was telling me that I should have just walked away, but I couldn't help myself."

"And look where it's gotten you now" Laura said as she picked up the bowls and placed them in the dishwasher. "It's still not too late to make a run for the door." But Henry knew he wasn't going anywhere. He was hooked and he knew it.

Laura looked at the clock over the stove and noticed it was now past midnight. "I should let you get some sleep," she said. "You've got to work in the morning. Thanks for the Rice Krispies. You were right, I feel much better now." She gave Henry a hug before she headed off to her bedroom.

On Wednesday morning, Henry was trying to be as quiet as possible as he showered and got ready for work because he didn't want to wake Laura. However, she poked her head out of her bedroom door just as Henry was going out the door of her condo. "I'm sorry I didn't get up in time to make you breakfast," Laura said. "I guess I was more tired than I thought. Did you find everything you needed?"

"Yes," Henry replied. "I just made myself some toast and I found some jam in your fridge." Henry stepped back inside the condo and gave Laura a hug. "So, do we have another midnight date tonight for a bowl of Rice Krispies?" Henry asked as he gave her a kiss on the forehead.

"Absolutely," Laura said.

* * *

When Henry arrived at the condo after work that day, Laura greeted him at the door but she didn't look quite as chipper as she had previously. "They moved my radiation treatment from 4PM to 3PM today," Laura said. "They said something about having to do maintenance on the equipment later in the day. Anyway, I find myself getting queasy two hours after my treatment. You can almost set your watch by it. If you don't mind, I'm going to go lie down for a while."

"No problem," Henry said, giving her a sympathetic look.

Laura emerged from her room about 10PM. She noticed Henry already had the bowls sitting on the table along with the box of Rice Krispies. There were also some fresh daisies in a vase on the table. Laura hadn't noticed that Henry had brought them with him when he had arrived after work, but the smile on her face let Henry know they were much appreciated.

They were just beginning their romantic dinner of Rice Krispies when Laura's phone rang. It was Samantha calling to see how Laura was doing so Laura didn't want to just blow her off. Laura indicated with her fingers that she would only be about two minutes, but Henry didn't believe her. He knew how women could talk, especially if they're best friends. After he finished his bowl of cereal, he headed off to his bedroom so they could talk in private.

Henry was sitting in bed under the covers reading a book when Laura knocked on his bedroom door over half an hour later. "Come in," Henry said.

Laura pushed the door open but continued to stand in the doorway. She pulled her bulky blue housecoat around her, feeling a little embarrassed to be there. "Sorry about that," Laura said. "I was really looking forward to our conversation over a bowl of cereal again tonight, but she just kept asking questions about the treatments and how I was doing. She's been my best friend forever."

"We can still talk," Henry said, tapping the pillow beside him.

"I can see what you're up to, you know," Laura said. "Come into my parlour said the spider to the fly," she said mockingly.

"You're safe," Henry said, "especially since you're wearing that blue armour you call a housecoat. Tell me about Samantha."

"Samantha and I have been friends since grade three," Laura said, slowly moving into the room and sitting on the end of the bed. "When my mom died, I practically lived at her place because my dad didn't seem to want to have anything to do with anyone, including me. We went to the same high school and when she got accepted at Arizona State, I decided I'd go there too. I had no idea what I wanted to be when I grew up and sort of stumbled in journalism while I was there. When I was offered the job with the Tribune after I graduated, I really debated whether to take it or not because Sam got a job in Toledo. Less than two months later, she showed up at my office to tell me she'd taken a job with the Lifestyles department at the Tribune. We're like two peas in a pod, never too far apart."

Samantha continued to tell Henry about her life. She glowed when she told him about her mother. She had a look of disappointment when she told him about her father. When she started to tell him about the day she discovered that she might have cancer, she crawled towards Henry because she desperately needed to be held.

"I was so afraid," she said. "Not so much that they'd found something. I was afraid that it would spread and they'd just keep removing more and more parts of me until there was nothing left."

Laura took off her blue housecoat and crawled under the covers with Henry, wearing just her nightgown. She squeezed him so tightly that it felt like she was inside his rib cage.

They made love, but this was different than the times in the hotel room at the Chicago airport. It was slower, almost like every part of their bodies was involved in the act. Not a word was spoken but they watched each other intensely as if their minds were communicating through a secret force field.

When they were both spent, they continued to hold each other. That's when Henry noticed that Laura had tears streaming down her face. He kissed her cheeks and wiped the tears away, but didn't really understand why she was crying.

"This is a first for me," Henry said. "I've never had a woman cry after I made love to her. Was I that good or that bad?"

Laura chuckled. "You were great," she said. "It's stupid really. I was thinking about when I was just about to go into surgery. I thought that this part of my life would be over once I had the surgery. I'm glad I was wrong."

"You know, I think women think much more about how they look than men do," Henry said. "Sure, we all gawk at the Playboy Playmate type of girls but we're attracted to all kinds of women, different shapes and sizes, different personalities."

"I just thought that guys would somehow see me as being....flawed," Laura said.

"Would you find me any less attractive if I only had one testicle?" Henry asked.

"Of course not," Laura replied.

"Right answer," Henry said.

"No way!" Laura said, rising up so she could look Henry in the eye.

"Check it out for yourself if you don't believe me," Henry said. "How did you think I knew so much about radiation treatments? I had to have fifteen treatments after my surgery as well, but I've been free and clear of cancer for over ten years now. But not to worry, you can still drive the car using only one cylinder."

"Your engine seems to work just fine," Laura said, reaching down to check out Henry's claim. "Yep, only one cylinder, but the engine seems to be all revved up and ready for action again."

They woke the next morning much later than planned and Henry knew he would be late for work yet again. To make matters worse, he would be leaving early today to catch a plane back to Toronto. He skipped breakfast altogether and raced to get his clothes stuffed into his carry-on bag. Laura was leaning up against the front door of her condo. She didn't want him to leave, but knew he had to. She was once again wearing her thick blue housecoat, but it wasn't tied closed like it had always been previously. Perhaps there was a chink in the armour.

"Are you sure you're going to be OK?" Henry asked as he scanned the room to make sure he'd packed all of his belongings. "I probably won't be back for a few weeks."

"I'll be fine," Laura said. "Samantha gets back today and said she'll be over tonight."

They hugged and kissed each other. Neither one wanted it to end, but Laura finally broke the embrace and opened the door. "Have a safe flight," she said as she watched

Henry walk down the hallway towards the elevators and closed the door.

"Love you," Henry said as he walked away.

Henry's heart skipped a beat when he realized what he'd said. He hadn't planned on saying the "L" word yet, it had just come out unexpectedly. But as he thought about it, he realized he did love her, even though they hadn't been together very long at all. He knew it in his bones. He wondered if he should go back to talk to Laura again. "You shouldn't just blurt out that you love somebody as you're walking away," he thought to himself. "It should be said much more romantically."

"Maybe she hadn't even heard him," he tried to rationalize to himself as he pressed the elevator button. Besides, he wouldn't know what to say now if he went back anyway.

Back inside the condo, Laura continued to lean up against the door. She had heard him and it had caught her completely by surprise. She pulled the drawstring of her thick blue housecoat tightly around her again.

"Love," she thought to herself. She wasn't sure she was ready for that.

*** CHAPTER 18 ***

When Henry got home later that night, he found David and Ashley sitting in the living room watching a movie. They were all cuddled up under a blanket, but lost the blanket and moved a little further apart when Henry walked in the room.

"Hello Ashley," Henry said.

"Hello Mr. Shaw," Ashley said. "How was your trip to Chicago?"

"Great," Henry replied. "How's Grandma doing?" Henry asked David.

"Not so good," David said. "She's been pretty depressed and she snaps at us for everything. Aunt Jenny has been trying to keep her busy but I'm not sure it's working."

"Try to cut her some slack. She's worried about Alan," Henry said. "Did anything else new happen around here?"

"Not much," David said. "Alex and I have been working with the trainer to put on some weight and build up our muscle strength. She's got us on a special diet and she works us really hard during our sessions. The coaches will be back a week from Saturday for our next tryout."

"Make sure you don't over-do it," Henry said. "The last thing you need right now is a pulled muscle."

"We hardly use much weight at all," David said, "but we do a lot of reps."

The credits were now rolling on the movie they had been watching. "Mind if I change this to the news?" Henry asked. It had been a few days since he'd seen any Canadian news and wondered if they would have any updates on the missing plane, but they didn't even mention it in their newscast. The news was dominated with stories about the President trying to push through new gun control legislation. There was story after story about the Republican-controlled House of Representatives and the Democrat-controlled Senate fighting with each other. The analysts didn't think there was much chance of getting anything done due to all of the political tap-dancing involved.

"These people are all so stupid," David said with disgust. "I can't watch any more of this. Ashley and I are going to go study in my room."

"You didn't tell me your trainer was a girl," Henry heard Ashley whisper to David as they walked away. Henry sensed that David was about to do some tap-dancing himself.

* * *

Henry was in the middle of breakfast the next morning when the phone rang. He was hoping it would be Detective Benedetti with some news about the missing plane, but it wasn't.

"Mr. Shaw?" asked the caller when Henry answered the phone.

Henry didn't recognize the voice. "Yes, this is Henry

Shaw."

"This is Manuel," said the caller, but Henry still didn't recognize who it was. "I'm the superintendent at your brother's apartment building. Do you remember we met a few weeks ago?"

"Yes," Henry said, finally connecting the dots. "What can I do for you?"

"I'm sorry to trouble you at this time. Your brother's rent is paid up until the end of the month but I've been told to start showing the apartment to new renters and I figured you might want to come and get your brother's possessions before we do. Or I can arrange to have them put into storage if you want, but there will be an extra cost for that. I'm so sorry. Have you heard anything more about your brother?"

"No, I haven't," Henry answered. "I'll make arrangements to come get Alan's stuff, but I'll have to get back to you later with the details."

Henry was still thinking about the logistics when David came into the kitchen for breakfast. "Do you think you and your brother could help me this Saturday load the stuff from Alan's apartment and take it to a storage facility?" Henry asked.

"Sure, but I don't know what Robert's up to this weekend."

"I'll check with him when he gets up," Henry said. "Don't say anything to Grandma about this. It might upset her." David nodded his agreement. He had already been walking around on eggshells trying to avoid anything that would upset her.

The next Saturday Henry rented a small cube-truck for the day to move Alan's possessions to a storage building located fairly close to Henry's neighbourhood. Robert had agreed to help them move the stuff as expected, as he always seemed to come through when needed. It helped that Robert was probably stronger than both Henry and David combined.

When they got to his apartment, it didn't take them long to load the furniture into the truck. They threw out all of the food as most of it had gone bad anyway. The biggest surprise was the number of clothes that Alan had. There must have been thirty suits, some of which looked like they'd never been worn at all, and numerous coats and jackets.

Manuel helped out a lot, even though he didn't have to. He even provided some large boxes that had hanging rods built into them that he said he'd kept after another tenant had moved in. As Henry was hanging the suits in the specially designed boxes, he came across one that had a tag with David's name on it. "For David's Graduation," the tag read. Henry could see from the label that it was a very expensive suit.

"David, I think this was meant to be given to you," Henry said, holding up the suit so that David could see it. David felt a lump in his throat.

As Henry put the clothes into the boxes, he kept watch for any others with special tags on them. Sure enough, he came across another tagged as "Robert's Christmas Present." This one looked like a very expensive leather jacket. There were several other shirts and jackets that had special tags on them that Henry set to the side. These were obviously presents that Alan had never gotten around to giving, and now probably never would. Henry tried to block that last thought out of his head, but failed.

They continued to load the truck with stuff to be taken to the storage facility. Henry put the clothes that he had set aside into his car, along with a few boxes of personal papers and a laptop computer, because he wanted to take them back to his house. It didn't take them long to unload the cube-van at the storage location and they were back home in what seemed like no time at all. Henry was glad to see that his mother wasn't home when they arrived.

"David, if it's OK with you, I'd like to put Alan's stuff from the car in the closet in your bedroom," Henry said. "Grandma won't be poking around in your room."

"That's fine," David said.

Later that night after his mother went to bed, Henry went to David's room and pulled the laptop out of the closet and set it up on the kitchen table. As soon as he turned it on, it prompted for a password. "Invalid password**********" displayed on the screen as Henry took his first guess at Alan's password. He tried the most common passwords like his birthdate, the name of their dog when they were kids, and even the name of Alan's first girlfriend from high school, but none of them worked. Henry showed it to Robert when he walked into the kitchen. Robert knew a lot about computers and always seemed to know how to fix computers when they did something strange.

"I can't seem to guess Alan's password," Henry said. "Do you think you can figure out a way to get around it?"

"Probably," Robert said. "Did you try entering "password" as his password? It's amazing how many people use that as their password."

Henry tried it. "Invalid password******" displayed on the screen.

Robert tried all of the key sequences he knew to try to get around the password prompt, like hitting the F2 or F8 keys, or holding the CTRL key while hitting other keys at the same time, but nothing worked. Robert noticed a small ID that appeared in the corner of the screen. It started off "US" but was followed by a series of letters and numbers that didn't make any sense.

"Leave it with me," Robert said. "I'll google some of the security sites to see if there's any information about how to get around it."

"Thanks," Henry said. "It looks like a pretty new computer so it may be useful to one of us."

It was several days later when Robert brought the laptop back to Henry. "Sorry Dad, but I couldn't get around the boot security on the laptop. When I searched the internet for any info on how to get around it, most of the hits seemed to indicate this is a military grade piece of software. Why would Uncle Alan be using security like this?"

"I have no idea," Henry answered. "It doesn't make any sense. Are you sure it's the same security software?"

"Pretty sure," Robert said. "I even put a question on one of the black hat blogging sites to see if anyone could give me any tips on how to get around it."

Henry looked concerned because he knew that those types of sites were frequented by hackers looking to share information about how to break into sites. "I'm not sure you should be going to those types of sites," Henry said.

"Don't worry. I don't use my real name on those sites. No one does. But if anyone shows up at the door asking for "Cow-pie", you never heard of him, OK?" Robert flashed a sly grin. "But one thing I learned," Robert continued, "was that you get a limited number of attempts to get the password correct before it thrashes the hard drive, making it useless. You know those stars that appeared at the end of the "Invalid password" message?"

"Yes," Henry answered trying to recall the exact message. "But I can't remember how many stars there were."

Robert showed Henry the laptop. "It looks like you've only got two attempts left," Robert said. "I'm sorry, but I probably used a few attempts myself trying to hack in, but I stopped when I found out how few attempts we have left."

"It's probably best if we just leave it alone for now," Henry said. "I'd hate to fry the hard drive and wipe everything out. Thanks for trying."

Robert agreed, but was still disappointed. He prided himself on being able to solve the problems that no one else could. He planned to keep digging, but didn't want to tell his dad.

*** CHAPTER 19 ***

On Saturday morning, Henry and David were up early as this was the day of the second tryout session for the Under-19 National Team. They were in the kitchen having breakfast when there was a knock on the door. As Henry approached the door he could see through the window that two men in suits were standing on his front steps. He assumed it would be Detective Benedetti and his partner so was caught by surprise when it wasn't.

"Are you Henry Shaw?" asked the first man.

"Who's asking?" Henry replied, seeming a little suspicious.

"I'm Officer McKee and this is Officer Wilson," said the first man. "We're with the RCMP. We're here to talk to you about your brother Alan." They flashed their badges but it was too quick for Henry to really see them.

"I've already told everything I know to Detective Benedetti and his partner," Henry said.

"We're aware of Detective Benedetti's ongoing investigation about the missing plane," Officer McKee said. "We're investigating a separate matter. We'd like to talk to you about some suspicious activities of your brother discovered by CSIS. Could we come inside to ask you a few questions?"

Henry knew that CSIS was the Canadian Security Intelligence Service but something about these officers didn't seem right. Before Henry could respond, they both stepped through the door and walked over to sit on the couch. Office McKee pulled a folder out of a briefcase he was carrying and put it on the coffee table, opened the cover and turned it so that Henry could see it. It showed a series of about a dozen pictures.

"Do you know any of these people and are you aware of any relationship between them and your brother?" Officer McKee asked.

Henry felt like he was being grilled and thought about asking them to leave, but relented and looked at the photos on the page. "Of course I know who some of these people are," Henry said. "Some of them are quite famous. That's Edward Bronson, and that's Frenchie Bouchard from the sports channel. I know my brother sold them some suits."

Henry scanned the rest of the pictures. All of them looked familiar to him, but he couldn't place exactly who they were. He thought one of the pictures looked like Donald McTavish, the managing partner from the Chicago firm, but Henry wasn't sure so didn't say anything. "Oh, that's David Suzuki," Henry said when he recognized another face. "He's the guy who used to host the science show on TV. I don't think my brother knows him at all."

Officer McKee turned the page to reveal another page of pictures. These were less familiar faces, but one picture almost jumped off the page. "That's Greg Blackwood," Henry said. "He works at the same law firm that I do. What's this all about?"

"We have some information that some or all of these

people, including your brother, have been involved in some kind of secret network," Officer McKee said.

"You think they're spies?" Henry asked, incredulously.

"We didn't say they were spies," Officer Wilson said, speaking for the first time. "We're not sure what they're involved in but we've had a request from a foreign government to investigate suspects within our jurisdiction. We're not aware of any solid evidence that Mr. Bronson and your brother were killed in a plane crash, just that they've gone missing."

"We understand you have a computer that belonged to your brother," Officer McKee said, continuing to press. "We'd like to take a look at it if we could."

Henry was growing more and more suspicious of these officers and began to worry they were trying to build a case against Alan to indicate that he was some sort of a spy. "Do you have a warrant?" Henry asked.

"We were hoping that you would be more cooperative," Office McKee said, "and that we wouldn't require one. But we can get one if required."

"Dad," said a voice from the hallway. "We really have to get going if I'm going to get to the tryouts in time." Henry had been so focused on the two officers that he had forgotten all about David and his soccer tryout. He wondered how much of the conversation David had overheard.

"I'm sorry gentlemen," Henry said, "but I'm going to have to ask you to leave. I have to take my son to a soccer tryout and he can't be late." Henry had said it with such authority that the officers knew that there was no point in trying to convince him otherwise.

"One last question," Officer McKee said. "Have you ever heard of anyone by the name of Goliath?"

Henry thought back to the night when he had the

strange conversation with his brother. "I've never heard that name before," Henry said, rising to show the officers to the door. He waited until he saw the officers back out of the driveway.

"OK, David," Henry shouted. "Get your stuff and I'll meet you at the car." As he said it, Henry went to the closet in David's room, pulled out the laptop and placed it on the kitchen table. When he started up the laptop, a familiar prompt appeared.

"Please enter your password:"

Henry hit the keys slowly. G-o-l-i-a-t-h and then hit the "Enter" key.

"Invalid password*" displayed on the screen.

"Damn!!!" Henry said in frustration. "Only one more chance," he thought to himself.

"What are you doing?" David asked, looking concerned.

"Don't worry about it," Henry said as he closed the laptop. "Let's go."

When they got to the car, David jumped into the passenger-side seat with his soccer bag on his lap and was checking to make sure he had everything. "Shit," David said. "I forgot my soccer ball." David raced back into the house, worried that he was going to be late.

As Henry waited in the car, he decided to call Greg Blackwood at the office to tell him what had happened. He wasn't surprised at all when Greg answered, even though it was early on a Saturday morning.

"Hi Greg, its Henry. I've got a bit of a situation."

"Hi Henry," Greg replied. "What's going on?"

Henry explained the situation about the two RCMP officers and the questions they had asked. "Did I do the right thing in asking them to get a warrant?" Henry asked.

"Absolutely," Greg replied. "They're not allowed to go on a fishing expedition without having some kind of evidence. Since it's the weekend, they probably won't be able to get a warrant until Monday at the earliest, and I'm not sure they'll even get it then. Do you have any idea what they think is on the laptop?"

"I have no idea," Henry said. "They talked about a secret network and had pictures about twenty people they're investigating including Edward Bronson, Frenchie Bouchard and David Suzuki. Your picture was one of them."

"Bizarre," Greg said. "Let me make some calls to see if I can figure out what they're up to and I'll get back to you. Is this the number I can reach you at?"

"Yes, but I'm just about to drive my son to his soccer tryout so just leave a message if I don't answer and I'll call you back."

Henry hung up the phone and glanced at his watch. They were going to have to hurry to have any chance of making the tryout on time. As he waited, Henry noticed a car with two men in it parked about two hundred yards down the street. He suspected it was the RCMP officers keeping an eye on him. Well they were going to be in for a real treat if they tried to follow him as he raced to David's soccer tryout. They were probably going to think he was trying to lose them.

"Sorry I took so long Dad," David said as he came running out of the house. "It took me a while to find it. It must have rolled under my bed."

David clutched his soccer bag on his lap as Henry threw the car into reverse and quickly backed out of the driveway. There was a sound of rubber as he accelerated down the street. Henry looked in his rear view mirror to see if the two men in the car were following. The car hadn't moved.

Henry drove quickly to try to get David to his soccer tryout in time. He tried to keep his speed about fifteen kilometres over the speed limit, hoping to make good time but not be fast enough for him to get pulled over by the police. He also sped through a few yellow lights that were more red than yellow. As he drove, he was constantly checking his rear-view mirror.

"It's OK Dad," David said. "I haven't seen any police yet." Henry didn't tell David that he was also checking to see if anyone was following them.

As they got closer to the soccer field in Vaughan, Henry determined that they were probably going to make it in time, so he slowed down a bit. They had been fortunate that traffic had been light. As they pulled into the parking lot, they were pleased to see a group of players standing outside chatting. The last thing David wanted was to be noticed as arriving late, so he quickly joined the group as if he had been there all along.

"I was starting to get worried about you," Alex said as he saw David approaching.

"Yeah, we were running a little late, but we made it on time," David said. David didn't elaborate on the reasons.

As they headed into the building, one of the coaches asked each player for their binder and ticked their name off on a list. David knew that his trainer had been making regular notations in his binder describing the progress he had been making in his strength conditioning sessions over the last few weeks.

Henry parked the car and was walking back toward the building when his cell phone rang. He could see from the call display that it was Greg. "Hi Greg. What did you find out?"

"Not much," Greg replied. "This is not my area of practice but I spoke to Ray Peterson from our criminal law division. Based on what we know so far, he doesn't think they'll get their warrant. He said you should call him if they come back to question you again. Sometimes just having a lawyer present forces them to behave themselves because they try to take advantage of people who don't know their rights." Before he hung up, Greg gave Henry the number for Ray Peterson's cell phone.

Henry headed into the building and sat with the other parents who were watching the soccer tryouts. Henry wasn't really paying attention to what was going on out on the field. His mind was racing. The questioning had really spooked him, particularly the part about Goliath. Henry felt guilty about lying to the officers. He never told lies, not even little white lies. Although he felt guilty about doing it, his gut feeling told him he had been correct in withholding that information, although he had no idea why.

"Your son's looking pretty good out there," said one of the parents who was sitting a few seats over from Henry. Henry didn't realize that the man was talking to him. "Your son's number 14 in the red jersey, right?" the man continued.

"Uh, yes that's my son David," Henry said, being pulled from his thoughts. "I'm Henry Shaw," he said, moving over a few seats to shake the man's hand.

"Bob Richardson," the man said. "That's my son Robbie, number 11 in white. Your son's got a lot of speed. Robbie's pretty fast himself but he said your son blew him away at the first tryout."

For the first time since he had arrived, Henry started to pay attention to what was going on out on the field. This was a lot different than the first tryout session and looked more like a regular soccer practice. There were still a lot of coaches out there, but this time they seemed to be focusing on teaching the skills of the game rather than just measuring everything through a series of tests.

Although he was biased, Henry agreed that David was

looking pretty good. David had always been very coachable and keen to learn new skills. He noticed that the coaches tended to use him when doing their demonstrations. One of the coaches made David fall down while demonstrating one of the skills and had made him look rather foolish. They could hear some of the other players laugh, even from the stands.

"Ouch," Bob said. "That's not fair. That coach used to play pro ball over in Europe. Kids are not going to see moves like that at this level."

They watched as the coach demonstrated what David had done wrong and showed him the correct footwork. David fell again the second time, but stole the ball from the coach on the third attempt. The coach grinned and gave David a high-five.

"Good for him," Bob said.

"David's not the type to give up," Henry said, puffing his chest out a little.

As they watched the rest of the practice, it became apparent that the skills being taught were at a much higher level than anything David had ever experienced previously. David had a huge smile as he came off the field at the end of the practice.

"You were looking pretty good out there," Henry said as David came towards the stands.

"Those guys are so good," David said. "I've got a bunch of stuff to work on over the next few weeks."

They continued to talk about the practice on the drive back home, which was done at a much more leisurely pace than the drive to the soccer field earlier that day. The stress from the events of that morning was gone, or was until they turned down the street to their house. Henry's heart skipped a beat when he saw the police car in his driveway with its flashers on. He saw Robert standing outside talking with a uniformed police officer. A few neighbours had gathered on their lawns trying to see what was going on.

Henry parked his car on the street and both Henry and David raced over to see what had happened. Robert looked relieved to see them. "What happened?" Henry asked as he approached.

"Someone broke into our house," Robert said. "I got home about twenty minutes ago and found the house ransacked. I went in through the back door and I think I heard them going out the front door when I was there. I called 9-1-1 and the police showed up a few minutes later."

"Are you OK?" Henry asked as he gave Robert a hug. It appeared that Henry needed the hug more than Robert.

"Did you see the suspects leaving?" the officer asked.

"No," Robert said. "I didn't see them at all, but I heard them running out the front door. They probably took off when they heard me come in the back door."

"What makes you think there was more than one person?" the officer asked.

"Just the sound," Robert said. "It sounded like two people, maybe three, running out the front door."

"Was there anyone else in the house at the time?" the officer asked.

"No," Henry interjected. "My mother's been over at my sister's place for the last few days. Robert was over at his friend Taylor's place last night for an all-night gaming tournament and David and I left the house earlier this morning to go to his soccer tryouts."

"What time was that, sir?"

"Probably a little after nine," Henry said. Henry looked at David for help. "David, what time did the officers leave this morning?"

"I think we left about ten after nine," David said.

"There were police officers here earlier this morning?"

the policeman asked, squinting his eyes as he became more suspicious.

"They were from the RCMP," Henry said. "At least, they said they were from the RCMP. I didn't get a real good look at their badges."

"Did you get their names?"

"Officer McKee was one of them," Henry said. "I can't remember the other officer's name right now, but it will come to me."

"It seems like you've had no shortage of police officers coming to see you lately," said a voice from behind Henry. Henry turned to see that it was Detective Benedetti. He whispered something to the uniformed officer, who headed inside the house as Detective Benedetti came over to talk to Henry.

"I heard this call come over the wire and thought I'd head over to see what all of the commotion was about. You said you were visited by a couple of RCMP officers this morning?"

"Yes," Henry said. "One of them identified himself as Officer McKee but I can't remember the other officer's name right now."

Detective Benedetti excused himself while he stepped away to make a call. "Officers McKee and Wilson" Detective Benedetti said when he returned. "They just confirmed that they visited you this morning, although they should have done me the courtesy of informing me they were coming to see you. They knew I had an ongoing investigation into your brother's disappearance. They said they're waiting for a warrant to get their hands on your brother's laptop. What's on the laptop, Henry?"

"To be honest, I have no idea," Henry said. "They were talking about some secret network or something. They showed me pictures of Edward Bronson, Frenchie

Bouchard and even David Suzuki, and said CSIS thinks they were all part of some secret network." Henry felt more trusting sharing information with Detective Benedetti than he had earlier with the two RCMP officers.

"Ah, CSIS," Detective Benedetti said. "They're usually involved in anything that's bizarre. I think they just sit around watching old episodes of the X-files to come up with some of this stuff. But something weird is going on. Your brother and Edward Bronson seem to have fallen off the face of the earth without a trace."

"Mr. Shaw, there are no signs of forced entry," the uniformed officer said as he came out of the house. "Do you normally lock your house when you leave?"

"Yes, but we were racing to get to the soccer tryout," Henry said. "David, do you remember whether you locked the house when you went back in to get your soccer ball?"

The look on David's face gave the answer. "Sorry Dad," David said, looking down at the ground. "I don't really remember, but I may have left it unlocked."

"Don't worry about it son," Henry said. "If they wanted in badly enough, they were going to get inside even if you did lock it."

"I was wondering if you could take a quick look around to see if anything is missing," said the uniformed officer. "Please don't touch anything because we still have to dust for fingerprints."

Henry stepped into the house along with Detective Benedetti and the uniformed police officer. "The laptop's gone," Henry said as soon as he stepped through the door. "I left it sitting on the kitchen table." Henry walked through the rest of the house. It looked like every drawer and closet in the house had been opened and the contents thrown about the room. "What a mess," Henry said, "but I don't see anything missing except for the laptop."

"They didn't touch any of the electronics," the uniformed officer said, pointing to the big screen TV and stereo equipment. There was even a new Blu-ray DVD player still in the box that Henry hadn't had time to set up yet.

"Since it occurred in the middle of the day and there wasn't much taken, I don't think this was a typical burglary," Detective Benedetti said. "They waited until they knew no one was here and were obviously looking for something specific."

"But why would they trash the place if all they were looking for was the laptop?" Henry asked, expressing his frustration at the mess they had created. "It was sitting out in the open on the kitchen table."

"Maybe they were looking for something more," Detective Benedetti said, "and your son came home before they could find it."

They headed back outside where Robert and David were waiting. "What do we do now?" Henry asked Detective Benedetti.

"It will take us several more hours to take pictures and dust for fingerprints, but I doubt we'll find anything," Detective Benedetti said. "We should be done sometime tonight but I'd suggest you find somewhere else to stay for the night if you can."

"I can probably stay at Alex's place," David said.

Robert indicated he could head back over to Taylor's place for the night and Henry said he'd be staying at his sister's place. Henry dreaded having to tell his mother about the incident because he knew it would upset her. He told the boys he'd pick them up early the next morning because he wanted to clean the place up at bit before his mother saw it.

"We need Robert and yourself to sign some statements

before you leave," Detective Benedetti said.

Robert was already talking to the uniformed officer and making some minor corrections to the report the officer had prepared. David was on his cell phone talking to Alex and confirming that he could stay at his place for the night.

"If you find anything else missing when you go through your stuff tomorrow, call me to let us know and we'll file an amendment to the report," Detective Benedetti said to Henry. "Believe it or not, this incident may actually help us figure out what happened to your brother and Edward Bronson. Something weird is going on. I just don't know what yet."

*** CHAPTER 20 ***

Henry received a call from Detective Benedetti later that night confirming that the police had completed their work.

"Did they find out who broke into your house?" Jenny asked when he got off the phone.

"No, I'm sure that will take some time, but they've completed dusting the place for fingerprints and gathering any other evidence at the scene," Henry replied. "He said we can take down the police tape surrounding the house and begin the cleanup process." Henry had been trying to update his sister about the break-in at his house without causing undue alarm to their mother, but he knew she had been listening to everything he said. To his surprise, she seemed encouraged by the news.

"I think this means that Alan's still alive," she said. "I don't know what he's got himself involved in but whoever broke into your house and stole his laptop obviously thinks it's going to help them find Alan. It probably has something to do with all of those stories he was telling us."

"I think that was just one of Alan's bipolar illusions," Henry said, but even he had to admit the thought had crossed his mind that some of those stories might not have been illusions after all.

The next morning Henry was up early and headed over to pick up Robert and David at their friends' places. He had told Jenny to delay bringing their mother over to the house until later if possible to give them time to clean up the place a bit. Henry and the boys started putting the clothes that had been strewn around the rooms back in their closets and drawers. It surprised them how quickly they had the house looking normal again.

"This doesn't look too bad," Henry's mother said as she came into the house. "It doesn't appear they broke anything. Did they take much?"

"The only thing that I know is missing is the laptop that was sitting on the kitchen table," Henry replied. "But let me know if you notice anything of yours missing."

Henry's mother went into her room and began taking all of the clothes that Henry had carefully folded and put away back out of the drawers and putting them into a laundry basket. She was going to wash everything she owned, as knowing that someone had pawed through her possessions made them feel dirty.

Henry confirmed with both Robert and David that they hadn't found anything else missing before he called Detective Benedetti. "It looks like the only thing they took was the laptop," Henry said. "I guess you can tell the RCMP officers that there's no point in them pursuing the warrant any more. You know, I thought I saw them parked down the street watching me when I left." Henry paused before continuing. "You don't think there's any chance they're the ones who took the laptop, do you? They didn't like that I was forcing them to get a warrant to get their hands on it."

"Not a chance," Detective Benedetti said. "I could tell

they were disappointed when I told them the laptop was taken. Besides, they do everything by the book."

After talking to Detective Benedetti, Henry called Greg Blackwood to let him know what had happened. Henry was surprised at how upset Greg seemed to be when he told him the laptop had been taken.

* * *

Henry was supposed to head to Chicago on Monday, but decided to delay it until the middle of the week to stay around the home-front a few more days. He could tell that everyone was a little spooked by the break-in, him included. Henry called Laura to let her know about the change in plans, although he didn't tell her about the break-in, just that something unexpected had come up. He had been calling her regularly over the last few weeks but had noticed she seemed a little distant on the phone. He suspected that she was getting run-down by her radiation treatments. Although she was tolerating them pretty well, Henry knew they took their toll on a person, both physically and mentally.

Henry arrived in Chicago on Wednesday and headed over to Laura's place after work. He was disappointed that he'd be staying at a hotel rather than at Laura's, but Samantha had moved back into Laura's second bedroom again when she returned from her business trip.

"Hi Henry," Samantha said as she opened the door to let Henry in.

"Hi Samantha," Henry said. "How's our girl doing?"

"She's doing pretty well," Samantha said. "She had her last radiation treatment last Friday so that's all done and over with. I'm trying to convince her to think about getting back to work, with limited success."

Samantha then pulled Henry in close to whisper

something to him. "Laura's been fitted with a prostheses and is really worried about how she looks so I need you to be really supportive of her when she comes out of the bedroom."

A few seconds later, Laura emerged from the bedroom wearing a regular blouse. It had been a while since Henry had seen her without her thick blue housecoat. She gave Henry a brief hug to greet him, but didn't look him in the eye. Instead, she retreated to the kitchen to empty the dishwasher. Henry and Samantha sat on the stools at the little breakfast bar that faced into the kitchen.

"So, I bet you're glad your radiation treatments are over with," Henry said, trying to start up a conversation.

"Yes, good riddance," Laura replied, continuing to put away the dishes. "Your suggestion about eating Rice Krispies sure helped getting over the nausea." Laura continued to avoid eye contact with anyone and seemed to be taking an incredibly long time putting the dishes away. Everyone knew what was going on, but no one wanted to acknowledge it.

"So, when do you think you'll be heading back to work?" Henry asked.

"I'm not sure," Laura replied.

It seemed to Henry that Laura was now just rearranging the dishes in the cupboard as the dishwasher had been emptied long ago. While Laura was facing the cupboard, Samantha tried to signal to Henry to say something nice about how Laura looked. Finally, Laura closed the cupboard doors and turned to face Henry. This was the first time since he'd arrived that she had looked directly at him.

"Nice rack," Henry said.

"Gawd!" Samantha said as she kicked Henry's stool sending it toppling, and Henry with it. "I said to say something nice and that's what you come out with? You insensitive clod!!!" It looked like she was going to punch him.

"Hey, that's the nicest compliment a guy can give," Henry said defensively.

Samantha turned back towards Laura with a worried look and was surprised to see Laura had burst out laughing. "I feel like I'm wearing a personal flotation device," Laura said trying to control her laughter. "I think they made it too big."

"Not possible," Henry said.

"Men and their fascination with big breasts," Samantha sighed in exasperation. "How would you like it if we talked about you guys in that way? We do, you know," Samantha continued, giving Henry an evil look. "Size – shape - whether it curves to the left or right."

Henry suddenly felt totally inadequate and subconsciously started to cross his legs.

"Don't let her scare you," Laura said, putting her hand on Henry's shoulder. "You have nothing to worry about in that department."

"You two perverts deserve each other," Samantha said, shaking your head. "I'm going to my room."

"Seriously," Laura said after Samantha had left the room, "do I look OK?"

"You look perfect," Henry replied, looking deeply into her eyes. "I've missed you."

"I've missed you too," Laura replied, hugging him tightly.

They spent the rest of the evening sitting on the couch talking and holding each other. Although they had only been apart a few weeks, they both were beginning to realize how much more complete they felt when they were together. Henry had been careful not to use the "L-word" again, but he was convinced now more than ever that this was real. And Laura didn't seem as afraid of the word as she had just a few weeks ago.

* * *

Henry was surprised when he received a call from Samantha the next day while he was at work. "I just thought I'd let you know that I've moved out of Laura's second bedroom and back to my own place. I wasn't going to until she was back at work, but she doesn't seem to be in any hurry to do that. I don't think she needs me to take care of her anymore."

"I'm sure she'll go back when she's ready," Henry replied.

"I'm not so sure," Samantha said. "She used to be so focused about her job but now it seems she's content to just sit around her place all day. I'm concerned that she may lose her job if she doesn't head back soon."

"Isn't she on some sort of short-term disability right now?" Henry asked.

"Yes, she is, but I'm not sure how much longer that will last," Samantha said. "Anyway, you won't have to worry about me chaperoning your visits with her anymore, but I'd appreciate it if you could encourage her to get back to work. I think it would be healthier for her in the long run."

Henry agreed and said he would do what he could. He raised the subject with Laura that evening after supper, but didn't make any progress as Laura quickly changed the subject. "So, what's been going on in your life back in Toronto?" Laura asked.

Henry hadn't told her anything about the situation with his brother. In fact, he liked being able to escape to Chicago to avoid thinking about it himself, but he started telling Laura about his brother and the missing plane.

"Edward Bronson's plane?" Laura asked. "You mean the guy who owns almost half the newspapers and TV stations in Canada?"

"One and the same," Henry said.

"How come I haven't heard anything about this?" Laura asked.

"I don't know," Henry answered. "It's been in all over the news in Canada and I even read a few reports on it in the Tribune here in Chicago." Laura suddenly realized she hadn't read a newspaper in weeks and even then, had only glanced at the front page.

Henry explained that his brother had sold Edward Bronson some suits, but he didn't think they really had a relationship other than that. When Henry told her about the visit he'd had from the RCMP, Laura was really intrigued.

"Then, last week our house was broken into and someone stole Alan's laptop," Henry continued. "That's why I delayed my trip to Chicago from Monday to Wednesday." Laura seemed deep in thought as if she was trying to solve a puzzle in her head. "I'm sorry," Henry said. "I guess I should have told you this earlier, but I knew you had your own problems to deal with."

When Henry left Laura's place that night, he could tell she was worried about him and his missing brother. Maybe he shouldn't have told her, he thought to himself.

Henry received another call from Samantha the next day at work. "What did you say to Laura last night?" Samantha asked as soon as Henry answered.

"Why – what do you mean?" Henry asked.

"Well, she apparently showed up at work before 6AM this morning researching some story," Samantha said. "She's been storming around the office commanding some of the junior reporters to make phone calls digging up additional information. I didn't even know she was back in the office until I heard a couple of guys in the elevator talking about it."

Henry told Samantha about his brother and Edward Bronson's missing plane. "Well, hang on to your hat partner," Samantha said, "because when she gets hold of a story, it's like a pit bull's got hold of your leg. If you kick your leg, he'll just bite you harder."

"I'm sorry," Henry said. "I guess I shouldn't have told her."

"Don't be," Samantha said. "It's good to have her back to her old self."

After he hung up the phone with Samantha, Henry tried to call Laura at the Tribune but they said she was out of the office. He tried her cell phone as well, but it went to voice-mail. It was much later in the afternoon when Henry's cell phone rang. He was pleased to see Laura's name appear on the call display.

"Where are you?" Laura asked.

"I'm actually on my way to the airport," Henry said. "My flight leaves in a little over two hours."

"OK, I'll meet you at the airport bar. I'm sure you know which one." She hung up before Henry could answer.

When Henry arrived at the airport bar, he didn't see Laura. He sat at the same table that he'd seen Laura and Samantha sitting at when he had first met them a few months earlier. When Laura arrived at the bar, she pulled out a file that had about an inch of paper in it and placed it on the table in front of Henry. It was a mixture of printouts of articles she'd found online, some hand-written notes and a multitude of yellow post-it notes.

"What's this?" Henry asked.

"It's everything I found out so far about your brother and Edward Bronson," Laura said. "The FBI does have

some evidence about a secret network of some kind and
Edward Bronson is definitely involved, but I couldn't find
anything on your brother."

"The FBI?" Henry asked.

"Yep. They first became aware of this network when a
new route for the oil pipeline from Canada to the U.S.
magically appeared while all of the politicians were still
fighting with each other as to where it was going to go and
who was going to pay for it."

"I remember a little bit about that," Henry said. "Some
senators and environmentalists were saying the proposed
route would endanger environmentally sensitive areas if
they ever had a rupture. Other senators were touting all of
the jobs it would create and how badly the U.S. needed the
oil. In the end, I think the President just vetoed it, didn't
he?"

"True, but remember how they magically came up with a
new route that avoided all of the environmentally sensitive
areas and a new funding formula within a few weeks after
that?" Laura asked.

"Yes, the President and a few state governors endorsed
that plan almost immediately," Henry said.

"Precisely, well the FBI believes that whole plan was
secretly put together by some scientists, environmentalists,
lawyers and some people from the oil industry and placed in
the lap of the President."

"David Suzuki," Henry muttered when he heard that it
involved scientists and environmentalists.

"Yes, I think that was one of the names I read in the
report," Laura said.

"How would this involve Edward Bronson or my
brother?" Henry asked.

"Apparently, Edward Bronson was financing this whole
thing," Laura said. "I guess he's got more money than he

knows what to do with. I couldn't find anything on your brother."

"Did you find anything that mentioned Goliath?" Henry asked. He hadn't told Laura that part the night before.

"Yeah, I read that somewhere in one of the reports," Laura said as she flipped through the pages trying to find where she'd seen it. "Here it is," Laura continued. "There's not much here but they think he's a courier. There's a whole bunch of couriers with code names like Goliath and Zeus. They're not directly involved, but they facilitate the exchange of information."

"I think my brother may have been Goliath," Henry said, now looking more worried than ever.

"Look, if it makes you feel any better, the FBI thinks that Edward Bronson has just gone into hiding, maybe along with your brother," Laura said, reaching out and putting her hand on top of Henry's.

"Why would they have to go into hiding?" Henry asked.

"Well, after their success with the pipeline project, they are apparently working on coming up with something on gun control," Laura said.

"America loves its guns," Henry said.

"And so does the National Rifle Association," Laura said. "The NRA spends a lot of money on lobbying and making sure that candidates from both parties that support their cause keep getting elected. They're not happy that there's some organization that they can't control working on the issue behind the scenes. The FBI thinks that some of the more radical people within the NRA found out that Edward Bronson is financing this network and they may be targeting him."

"Can't the FBI protect them?" Henry asked.

"They don't know where they are either," Laura answered.

"Maybe if you print this story, they could come out of hiding," Henry said, grasping for a solution.

"I can't use any of this information in a story. My source at the FBI told this to me in confidence."

"Sounds like you've got quite the source."

"The best," Laura said, looking away. "I haven't spoken to him in years." After a few seconds, Laura turned back and looked Henry in the eye. "He's the guy I used to live with," Laura confessed. "I wasn't sure he'd even talk to me when I called, but he did. I told him about you. It's funny - it was only after I told him about you that he spilled the details. I don't plan on contacting him again. I can't put him in that position again because he'd lose his job if anyone ever finds out he told me what he did. His job is more important to him than anything."

"Apparently not," Henry thought to himself.

The last call for Henry's flight came over the speakers in the airport. They hugged each other tightly and it was evident that neither one of them wanted to break the embrace.

"I'm glad you suggested we meet here," Henry said kissing Laura. "This will always be my favourite airport bar."

"Mine too," Laura said.

As Henry flew back to Toronto that evening, he felt a little more optimistic about his brother's situation. "Maybe the FBI is right and they've just gone into hiding," he thought to himself.

* * *

The room was in total darkness except for a tiny sliver of light that crept in alongside the curtains that were being used to block anyone from outside from seeing what was going on inside the room. A man reached inside the bag that was filled almost to capacity, lifted the long piece of plastic that covered the bottom of the bag and slid a computer out from underneath it. The bag had been kicked around a lot on its latest journey and there was no way of telling if the computer would still work.

When he turned the computer on, the screen lit up the room revealing a familiar profile.

"Please enter your password:" prompted the screen.

He entered the complex combination of letters and numbers slowly and carefully hit the "Enter" key.

After a few seconds, "Welcome, Goliath" flashed on the screen.

After a few more seconds, a second message appeared.

"Package ready for delivery."

The cursor scrolled down further and a single ">" prompt appeared waiting for his response.

"Problems encountered. Unable to deliver at this time," he typed.

When he entered "EOT" to signal the end of transmission, the computer shut-down almost immediately and the room returned to darkness.

*** CHAPTER 21 ***

Henry was pleased to see David sitting at the kitchen table the next morning when he went in for breakfast. "You're up early," Henry said.

"Yeah, the coach is letting Alex and I use the gym at school early in the morning," David said. "He really wants us to make the U-19 team and has been working with us to improve our skills."

The season for the high school soccer team had been over for several weeks now, so Henry realized the coach was going well above and beyond his normal responsibilities. With snow now on the ground, there weren't too many places where David and Alex could work on their skills so knowing someone with a key to the gym was a real bonus.

"Dad," David said, "could you ask Grandma to stop barging into my room without knocking? She burst into my room a few nights ago when Ashley and I were in there studying. It's embarrassing."

"Are you sure you were just studying?" Henry asked. "Should we be having another conversation about sex?"

"Why, have you forgotten something?"

"Don't be smart!"

"We're not having sex," David said, feeling somewhat embarrassed at having this conversation. "It would be impossible in this house, especially with Grandma around."

Henry thought Grandma knew exactly what she was doing. He remembered when he was a teenager and how she always seemed to be around when he least wanted her there, but her presence probably saved him from getting into a lot of trouble.

"I'll talk to her," Henry said. "But, take things slow. The last thing you want right now is for someone to get pregnant."

As David left the kitchen, Henry felt like such a hypocrite. Here he was telling his son to think about controlling his urges and about protected sex and he realized those thoughts had never even crossed his own mind in his encounters with Laura. He made a mental note to have a conversation with Laura about the subject.

* * *

A few weeks later, Henry and David were once again heading off to Vaughan for another session with the U-19 coaches. Henry paid more attention to the practice this time and noticed that both David and Alex's skills had seen a marked improvement over the last several weeks. The coaches gathered the players together on the far side of the field at the end of the practice and spoke to the players for quite a while. When the practice was over, David and Alex walked over to the sidelines together. "Congratulations," Alex said as he gave David a hug, and then headed off to meet his parents.

David was beaming. He was trying to act cool and nonchalant, but Henry could tell that David was excited.

"What was that about?" Henry asked.

"They asked me to go with the team to Florida to play a friendly match against the U.S. team," David said, trying to control the excitement in his voice. "It's being held over the Christmas break so it won't interfere with school. Can I go?"

"I don't see any reason why not," Henry said, giving David a hug.

"The coaches said I probably won't actually get into the game. Most of the guys going were on the team last year. There are only two new players, myself and Tim Duncan. I'm not sure if you remember him. He's the guy I played against from North Bay."

"Number eighteen," Henry said. "Yeah, I remember him."

David sensed from Henry's tone that he wasn't a fan of number eighteen. "Tim's not a bad guy, once you get to know him."

They continued talking while they walked to the car. "They also introduced a new coach today," David said. "Nigel Smith. I don't really know anything about him but he's from England and apparently a pretty big deal. He knows guys like Wayne Rooney and David Beckham."

* * *

Over the next few weeks, they made plans for the trip to Florida. David seemed a little embarrassed over the fuss that everyone was making and kept reminding them that he wasn't expected to play and would be just sitting on the bench for the entire game. But Henry decided to make a holiday out of it and both he and Robert would be heading down to Florida for the game. They also planned to take in a Miami Dolphins game the next day. Grandma was still worried about Alan and said she wasn't that keen on travelling, so wouldn't be coming along.

Henry was excited about the trip, but also a little nervous. He'd invited Laura down and this would be the first time the boys would be meeting her. Henry had already told them about Laura, but had deliberately kept it low key and told them it was just someone he had met in Chicago. He told them Laura was going to be in Florida on business which was really stretching the truth. Laura had arranged the business part of her trip around the holiday, not the other way around.

When Henry and Robert arrived at the soccer stadium in Fort Lauderdale, they were surprised that there was hardly anyone there. "Are you sure we're in the right place?" Robert asked.

"I think so," Henry said. "The game is supposed to be played at the home stadium of the Fort Lauderdale Strikers and I think this is the place." As they moved further into the stadium, Henry was pleased to see David and the rest of the team out on the field doing their warm-ups. David had gone to the stadium a few hours earlier with the rest of the team on the team bus.

"Pick a seat, any seat," Robert said as they climbed into the stands. There seemed to be about three groups of people in the stands, parents and friends of the Canadian team, parents and friends of the U.S. team, and coaches and scouts. There were only a few hundred people in total. Henry recognized a few of the parents from the tryouts and started heading toward that group of people.

Although he probably didn't really need them, Henry had brought along a pair of binoculars and started using them to get a closer look at David. When the players headed back into the dressing room after their pre-game warm-up, Henry started using them to scan the rest of the stadium. He noticed several people up in the press boxes with their own binoculars watching players on the field and was surprised to see that Frenchie Bouchard was one of them. The bright gold sports jacket he was wearing was a dead give-away. Henry thought it was strange that Frenchie would be covering such a small event.

Henry continued to scan the rest of the stadium and was surprised when he saw two men in suits who also had binoculars, and they appeared to be pointing their binoculars directly at him.

"Can I borrow the binoculars?" Robert asked. It was obvious he was getting bored.

"Sure," Henry said as he handed them to Robert. Robert only used them for a few seconds before giving them back to Henry. When Henry looked again where the two men in suits had been standing, they were gone.

* * *

Inside the dressing room, the new coach from England, Nigel Smith, was introducing Frenchie Bouchard to all of the players. To these kids, Frenchie was a bit of a celebrity because they all watched the sports channel. He made sure the camera-man got a shot of each player. "You never know when one of you guys will be featured on our highlight of the night. Make something good happen out there today!"

When the coach introduced David to Frenchie, Frenchie did a double-take. "You must be related to Alan Shaw, because you're the spitting image of him. I wouldn't look as good as I do without your uncle's help," he said, modeling his bright gold sports jacket. Frenchie turned to his camera-man and told him to turn off the camera for a minute. "Your uncle spoke about you quite a bit and is quite proud of you. I was so sorry to hear about his disappearance. Have you heard anything further?"

"I don't think so," David said. "The police keep my dad updated but I don't think they've come up with anything yet."

"Well, we're all praying for him," Frenchie said, giving David a hug.

Frenchie continued through the dressing room making sure he spoke to every player. Afterwards, David noticed that Frenchie spent a lot of time talking to their new coach. David also saw the coach give Frenchie an envelope which Frenchie quickly placed inside his sports jacket.

* * *

Out in the stands, Henry was pleased to see Laura climbing the stairs towards them. "This is my oldest son Robert," Henry said as he introduced them. "Laura is a friend of mine from Chicago who's down here on business. She's a journalist who works for the Chicago Tribune."

Henry realized he was talking too much, but he was nervous and couldn't seem to stop. Finally, Laura saved him from himself. "Boy, it's sure hot up here in the stands," Laura said. "I was going to get a drink but all of the concession stands seem to be closed."

"The game won't be starting for a while," Henry said. "I'll go see if I can find us something to drink. Do you want bottled water or a soft drink?"

"It doesn't matter," Laura said, "as long as it's wet and cold."

"I'll have a coke if you can find one," Robert said.

Robert and Laura started talking as Henry headed off in search of refreshments. It took Henry a lot longer than he expected as they only had a few concessions open due to the small number of spectators. He returned about twenty minutes later with a coke and two bottles of water.

"Sorry it took me so long," Henry said. "I had to walk

almost around the whole stadium before I found a concession that was open. So what have you two been talking about while I was gone?" Henry didn't give them any time to answer before he started talking again. "Did Laura tell you about the business that brought her down to Florida?" Henry asked Robert.

"The jig is up," Laura interrupted. "Robert knows that the business trip is just a ruse and that we're more than just friends. You know, your son would make a very good investigative journalist himself because he had me spilling the truth within a few seconds after you left."

Henry looked a little sheepish at being caught. "How long have you known?" Henry asked Robert.

"We knew you were spending a lot more time in Chicago than you really needed to," Robert said. "We figured you must have had a pretty good reason," Robert continued, teasingly bumping his shoulder against Laura's.

"Which one is David?" Laura asked, pointing to the players out on the field.

"He's number 14," Henry said. "He's just putting the yellow bib over top of his jersey because he's a substitute. He said he probably won't get to play at all during the game but he's still thrilled to be here."

They watched the game, but it was actually a pretty boring game to watch, even for the parents. The only ones who seemed to be following the game closely were the group of coaches and scouts.

At half-time, Henry noticed Frenchie Bouchard on the sidelines interviewing the new Canadian coach. They had done the interview right in front of the stands where there were the most people. Henry knew they had done this so it would look like the game was well attended when it aired on the sports channel back in Canada. Frenchie departed right after the interview and didn't stay around for the second half of the game. Henry suspected that Frenchie had only come to the game for that interview.

The second half of the game was as boring as the first half and as expected, David had sat on the bench the entire time. The game ended in a one-one draw and the players started exchanging jersey's after the final whistle blew.

"What are they doing?" Laura asked.

"Sometimes in games like these, the players exchange jersey's with players from the other team," Henry said. "It's like it's a souvenir of the game."

Henry was hoping to introduce Laura to David after the game, but he had simply waved at them as he ran off the field with the rest of the team. "Sorry about that," Henry said. "But you'll get to meet him tomorrow at the Dolphins game."

"I'm looking forward to it," Laura said, giving Henry a kiss on the cheek. "Well, I gotta run. Nice meeting you Robert."

"So, what did you think of Laura?" Henry asked Robert after Laura had left.

"I like her," Robert said. "More importantly, what do you think of Laura?" Henry didn't answer. "I thought so," Robert said.

As Henry and Robert headed out of the stadium together, Henry had the feeling they were being watched. He scanned the far side of the stadium looking for the two men in suits who he had seen earlier, but didn't see them anywhere. But they had been watching everything that was going on.

One of the two men in suits was standing in the shadows along the side of the stadium. He was a big man in his late forties who was dressed like he was a successful businessman. But he wasn't, he simply looked after their interests. He flipped open his cell phone and hit the buttons to dial one of his contacts. "It's Carter. Yeah, he's here at his son's soccer game along with his other son and some woman. There's no sign of his brother. Despite what your source at the FBI said, I don't think there's any way Bronson's plane could have made it. We did quite a number on that plane."

As he listened to the response over the phone, his partner came over to join him. Cuccinelli, or Cujo as he was more commonly known as was in his early thirties and also dressed like a successful businessman. He looked quite friendly, or he did until he took off his sunglasses. There was something about this man's eyes that left no doubt that he was evil to the core. Carter handed him the phone.

Cujo listened intently to the person on the other end before he spoke. "Yeah, I've been tracking Bouchard. He's definitely involved. It will be difficult because he's rarely by himself, but we'll take care of it."

He put his sunglasses back on and the two men casually strolled out of the stadium. As they walked by one of the large garbage containers that lined the pathway, Carter stopped to tie his shoe while his partner dumped their burner phone into the trash.

*** CHAPTER 22 ***

Henry, David and Robert talked about the game at the hotel later that evening. "I hope you guys weren't too bored," David said. "I told you that it was no big deal and you didn't have to come."

"I wouldn't have missed it for the world," Henry said.

"Hopefully the Dolphins game will be a little more exciting tomorrow," Robert said. "That's the game I'm really looking forward to."

"Laura used her connections with the Tribune to get us some pretty good seats," Henry said. "It's too bad you didn't get to meet her today David."

"Sorry about that," David said. "I thought it was best that I stay with the team."

Henry turned on the TV in the hotel room and flipped the channels until he came to the local news station. The lead story showed the President talking about his gun control legislation and how optimistic he was that he'd be able to get the required votes to pass it in both the Senate and the House of Representatives. It was followed by interviews of several other politicians who said there was practically no chance it would get approved.

"Can we watch something else?" David asked. "I can't stand listening to these politicians."

Henry turned to Robert to see if he minded, but could see that he was listening to music on his iPod and wasn't even watching the TV. Henry started flipping through channels but stopped when he came across the Florida Panthers hockey game. The Toronto Maple Leafs were in town to face the Panthers and the announcers were doing their pre-game show. The bright gold sports jacket of one of the announcers could only be Frenchie Bouchard.

"He came into the dressing room today before the game to wish us all good luck," David said. "I actually got to talk to him for a while."

"I met him at a hockey game in Toronto," Henry said. "Alan introduced me to him when he was dropping off some new sports jackets." They spent the rest of the night watching the hockey game which resulted in a win for the Leafs.

The next day Henry and the boys met Laura at the football stadium to watch the Miami Dolphins who were taking on the New York Jets. Whereas there were very few people at the soccer game the day before, there were thousands of people outside of the football stadium and it took them a while to locate her.

"Hi Laura," Henry yelled when he finally saw her. He could tell she couldn't hear him so they pushed their way through the crowd to get closer. She didn't see him until he was almost right in front of her. "Hi Laura," Henry said again. "You remember Robert from yesterday and this is my youngest son, David."

"Nice to meet you," Laura said, reaching out her hand. She barely got an acknowledgement from David, but that may have been due to him getting jostled by the people trying to get by them. "I've got the tickets," Laura said, holding them up. "We should probably get inside and out of this chaos."

"Great seats," Henry said when they finally got to their seats.

"Yeah, one of the sports-writers at the Tribune called in a few markers from the guys at the Miami Herald to get these," Laura said. "I think I'll be taking the guy to lunch every day for a month."

"These are great," Robert said. "Thanks so much."

David didn't say a thing until Robert secretly gave him an elbow to the ribs. "Thanks," David said, but quickly turned his focus back to the field where the players were going through their pre-game warm-ups.

Henry was about to say something to David, but Laura stopped him. "Why don't you and Robert go get us some drinks," Laura said. "It will give David and me a chance to get to know each other." Henry gave Laura a worried look, but relented to her request.

"I was glad to get to go to your soccer game yesterday," Laura said after Henry and Robert had left. "Your dad's quite proud of you for being selected to the National team."

"It's no big deal," David said. "I just sat on the bench for the whole game." David still hadn't really looked at her.

"Maybe you'll get to play in the next game," Laura said. "When is the next game?"

"We play an exhibition game against a team from England here in Florida in the middle of February and another game against the U.S. team in Washington at March Break."

"That should be exciting," Laura said, but she didn't get a response. "Are you a Dolphins fan?" Laura asked, trying to keep the conversation going.

"Not really," David answered, shutting it down.

After an awkward silence of a minute that seemed more like an hour, David looked over at Laura. He could tell she was important to his dad and because of that, he decided he should make more of an effort to like her. Even though he'd just met Laura, he could tell that it was important to her as well.

"I'm a big NFL fan," David said, "but I've never really followed the Dolphins. Boy, they sure love Dan Marino down here. It seems like he's in every commercial for cars and restaurants."

Laura lit up when David started the conversation again. "I know what you mean," Laura said. "To be honest, I'm not even sure why he's so famous," she whispered to David, making sure none of the fans around them could hear her.

Henry and Robert arrived a few minutes later with drinks and snacks. The football game was one-sided with Miami winning easily, but that seemed to get the crowd more into a party mood. If there were any fans of the opposing team there, they were keeping that fact to themselves.

Henry hadn't noticed the man that had followed him from the concession stand and up into the stands. He looked like any other fan at the game, except his sunglasses hid the fact that he was watching Henry more than he was watching the game. He kept going up the stands until he sat down beside his partner about fifteen rows behind where Henry was sitting. "I don't know why the boss wants us to keep following this guy," Cujo whispered to his partner. "I think his brother is long-gone."

"We just do as we're told," Carter whispered back. "Someone is using that laptop. If Bronson and his brother somehow survived their little plane ride, the boss thinks he'll eventually contact this guy and that will lead us directly to Bronson."

After the game, David headed off with Robert to buy a Dolphins jersey. Although he wasn't a Dolphins fan, he was trying to build a collection of jerseys from every team. This gave Henry and Laura some time to be alone, if you could call being among sixty thousand people being alone.

"I really like your boys," Laura said, giving Henry a hug. "Robert's warm and friendly and I can tell he's the type who would never let anyone down. David's a bit more of a puzzle, but I like him as well. He seems like he's carrying the weight of the world on his shoulders. He's going to do great things – I don't know what, but I can just tell."

"I'm glad you liked them," Henry said.

"Let me know if they liked me," Laura said.

"How could they not?" Henry said, giving her a big kiss.

*** CHAPTER 23 ***

The next week Henry was off to Chicago again. Since the merger had been completed long ago and things were running smoothly, he was now only going there about twice a month. He really looked forward to seeing Laura on each trip and the weeks they were apart seemed to drag on forever.

They had been talking more and more about their relationship. Neither of them liked the long distance aspect, but they didn't know what to do about it. Laura was now back into her job with the same dedication and enthusiasm that she used to have, so she really didn't want to leave Chicago. And Henry loved his job and his family life so couldn't see himself making any changes either, at least not at this point.

"Why did you pick me?" Henry asked as they lay in bed that night.

"What do you mean?"

"That night in the bar at the Chicago airport," Henry said. "You could have any guy you wanted. Why did you pick me?"

"I don't know," Laura said. "Sam and I had been there for quite a while. She kept trying to talk me out of it. We must have talked about twenty different guys that we saw in that bar that day. Some of them were downright creepy. We could hear you talking with your friends and I liked your voice. I liked your hands."

"My hands?" Henry asked. "I've heard of people with a foot fetish but I've never heard of anyone with a hand fetish."

"You asked," Laura said laughing. "Sam liked you too, but I think she thought you were the most likely to turn me down. She really didn't want me to go through with it. In fact, we were just about to leave and call the whole thing off when I saw your friends head off to catch their flight. When I saw you sitting alone at the bar, I decided to go for it. I had no idea what I was going to say when I got there."

"Yeah, I thought you were a hooker," Henry said, "except they're usually a little more subtle."

"I didn't mean to say that," Laura said continuing to laugh. "In fact, Sam and I had talked about me just sitting at the bar and letting the guy make the first move. When I touched you on the arm and you turned to look at me, I just blurted it out."

"Any regrets?" Henry asked.

"None," Laura said.

* * *

Over the next few weeks, David and Alex continued to work hard during their training sessions, building their "core strength" as the coach called it. David had once again been asked to travel with the team back to Florida for their friendly game against the team from England, although he was not expected to get any game time. Henry wanted to fly down to Florida to attend the game but David had talked him out of it.

Henry was at home that evening half asleep in front of the TV when the phone rang. "Hi Dad," David said. He couldn't hide the excitement in his voice.

"Hi David. How did your game go today?"

"I got to play," David said. "I wasn't supposed to, but Tim hurt his knee when he crashed into their keeper and he got a yellow card on the play. The coach was pretty mad at Tim and pulled him out of the game, moved Doug up to striker and I got to go in at midfield."

"Good for you!" Henry said. "Oh, I wish I had been there to see it."

"I only got to play for the last five or six minutes of the game and I didn't even touch the ball once."

"Did you guys win?" Henry asked.

"No, we got waxed," David said. "Those guys are so good. They were up three-nil at the half and I think they played their second-stringers for the second half, but we still didn't get anywhere close to scoring a goal. They beat us five-nil. It's easy to see why they're ranked number four in the world and we're still trying to break into the top fifty. The coach wasn't happy with our play."

Henry regretted that he'd let David talk him out of not flying down for the game. He would not make the same mistake for their next game in Washington.

David flew back with the rest of the team the next day. When Henry got home from work that day, he found David in his room pinning the jerseys from the other teams on his wall with help from his grandmother.

"This is the jersey I got from the U.S. team," David said.

"It's a little crooked," Grandma said. "Raise it up a bit on the left side."

"And this is the jersey I got from the English team," David said. "Turgott was one of their best players."

Grandma noticed that the threads on one of the letters of his name had come unravelled. "Here, give me that," she said. "It will only take me a minute to fix it." She gave it back to David after she fixed it, along with a little sewing kit she always carried with her.

"You should keep this with your own soccer jersey in case it gets ripped," Grandma said giving him the sewing kit. "I've seen the way those players hold and tug on each other's jersey. They should get a penalty when they do that." David pinned the England jersey up on his wall beside the one from the U.S. team.

Henry noticed a World Cup soccer ball sitting on the shelf. "When did you get the World Cup soccer ball?" Henry asked. "I've been trying to find one of those for months."

"That's actually the ball that Uncle Alan got for me," David said. "I've been using the ball at practice and I was out in the driveway kicking it against the garage when I noticed the Goliath logo was starting to peel off the ball. I thought I had wrecked the ball, but when I pulled off the Goliath logo it had the Adidas logo underneath. I thought I should keep the ball because Uncle Alan..."

David stopped in mid-sentence and wished he would have stopped talking sooner. He could see the tear come into his grandmother's eye before she quickly left the room.

"I'm sorry," he said. "I didn't mean to..."

"It's OK David," Henry said. "She's still hoping they'll find Uncle Alan. We all do." Henry followed his mother down the hall to try to console her.

* * *

As the weeks went by, Henry found himself thinking less and less about his missing brother. At the start, detective Benedetti would call him every day or two giving him updates on the progress of their investigation. It had now been over two weeks since Henry had last heard from him so he decided to give him a call.

"Sorry," Benedetti said. "I should have been keeping you updated but, to be honest, we've got nothing new to report. We've followed up every lead and come up with nothing, with the missing plane or on whoever broke into your house and stole the laptop. The RCMP are still investigating the matter as well but have got nothing so far. They did say the FBI is picking up chatter that the secret network that Bronson was involved in is still active, so we're hopeful that some of their work will lead us to Bronson and your brother."

Henry thanked him for the update and then called his sister to pass on the information. "I'm getting less and less confident that they're going to find Alan," Jenny said. "How's mom taking all of this?"

"She's probably the most optimistic of all of us," Henry said. "I wish I shared her view."

*** CHAPTER 24 ***

Henry sat in the Toronto airport waiting for his flight to Washington. Since it was the beginning of March break, the airport was much busier than normal. The U19 National Team, including David, had already headed down to Washington the previous day by bus. The coach had said a road trip by bus was a good way for the team to bond together but Henry suspected that cost was also a factor in the decision.

Henry was surprised when he saw Greg Blackwood walking toward him. "Hi Greg," Henry said. "Where are you off to?"

"Washington. I'm meeting with some clients over the next few days."

"I'm heading to Washington myself. My son David plays for the U19 National Soccer Team and they've got an exhibition game against the U.S. team tomorrow." Greg already knew that David played for the national team as Henry had been talking about it for months, but that didn't stop Henry from continuing to brag about it.

A few minutes later, they called for boarding to begin for

the first class passengers. "What hotel are you staying at?" Greg asked.

"Holiday Inn," Henry answered.

"I'm staying at the Hilton," Greg said, "but I think they're close to each other. After we get off the plane, I'll wait for you so we can share a cab."

"That would be great," Henry said.

By the time Henry boarded, he could see that Greg had already been served a drink and was on the second section of the complimentary newspaper. Henry also saw Frenchie Bouchard sitting in first class and he said hello to Henry as he went by, but Henry noticed he said hello to practically everyone else as well. Henry doubted he remembered that Alan had introduced them several months ago. Henry continued his journey back to seat 26B.

When Henry got off the plane, he saw Frenchie renting a car and wondered whether he would see him at David's soccer game, or whether he was in Washington to cover a hockey or basketball game.

Greg waved to Henry as he approached. When they got outside of the airport, they were surprised to see how long the lineup was at the taxi stand. Greg signalled to a limo driver who was parked in a separate area and the driver immediately sprinted over to take their bags. "I can't believe how busy it is," Greg said. "It costs about $20 more to take a limo but I think it's worth it on a day like today."

Henry had the sense that they were being watched and scanned the crowd of people wondering if he would see the two men in suits that he had seen at the soccer game in Florida. He didn't see them, but there was no shortage of men in suits who seemed to be monitoring the situation. "Welcome to Washington, the city of spies," Henry thought to himself.

It took them forever to get through the Washington

traffic and to their respective hotels. In the end, it probably cost them less by paying a flat fee for the limo rather than watching the meter tick off the dollars in a taxi while stuck in traffic. "Best of luck to your son in his soccer game," Greg said when he dropped Henry off at his hotel.

* * *

Back at the airport, Frenchie signed the vehicle rental agreement and the agent handed him the keys which had a tag indicating the car was a silver Chrylser 200, but Frenchie was having a hard time finding it in the rows and rows of rental cars. He was pleased when one of the agents offered to help.

"We've got so many cars coming and going, it's hard to keep track of them all," the agent said as he walked with Frenchie down one of the rows of vehicles. "The cars that are ready to go out again are normally found in this row."

Frenchie was surprised at how old this agent was as the car rental places tended to hire kids fresh out of school for this type of job because they paid them practically nothing. They didn't have any luck locating the vehicle and Frenchie glanced at his watch noting the time.

"You know you can take any car you like from this section," said the agent. "It doesn't have to be the Chrysler 200 indicated on your reservation. We just had a Dodge Charger come back that I just cleaned up. I can let you take that vehicle for the same price."

Frenchie's eyes lit up when he saw the bright red Charger. He'd always been interested in muscle cars and this car seemed to match his personality. "Deal," he said as he exchanged the car keys with the agent. As he headed out of the rental parking lot, Frenchie gunned the engine and liked the full-throttle sound. "This is going to be fun," he thought to himself.

When the agent saw Frenchie pull out of the parking lot, he quickly pulled off the rental company's uniform and dumped it in the trash. His partner came out of the shadows and handed Carter his regular suit jacket. They both jumped in their car and headed out of the parking lot following Frenchie.

"That was easier than I thought," Carter said to his partner. "But we better follow him to make sure things go as planned."

* * *

Henry grabbed some supper at a little restaurant that was beside the Holiday Inn. The flight and sitting through traffic had drained him of energy so he just headed to his room and turned on the TV. The lead story on the news that night was that the President's new gun control legislation had just squeaked through the Democratic-led Senate. The big challenge now would be getting it through the Republican-led House of Representatives, which now appeared that it would be a much closer vote than first expected.

"It's a good thing David's not watching this," Henry thought to himself. "He hates this kind of politics."

Henry grabbed the remote control and flipped through the channels until he got to the local sports channel which was preparing to broadcast the Washington-Montreal hockey game.

"We'd like to send out our best wishes for a speedy recovery to Frenchie Bouchard," the announcer said. "He was involved in a car accident late this afternoon on his way to the arena and is in critical condition in a Washington hospital. We'll be providing further updates on his condition as we receive them."

"Oh my God," Henry thought.

* * *

The curtains of the room had been closed as tightly as they could, but the light from the flashing neon sign outside the hotel lit up the room with an eerie throb that seemed to be in synch with the man's own breathing which was much faster than normal.

"Please enter your password:" prompted the screen.

The man pulled something out of his back pocket and carefully entered the complex combination of letters and numbers written on it into the computer and hit the "Enter" key. After a few seconds, "Welcome, Goliath" flashed on the screen.

The cursor scrolled down further and a single ">" prompt appeared.

"Transfer of package failed. Pursuing other options," he typed.

"Other options," he thought to himself. Even he didn't know what that meant, but he knew he had to come up with something. He wasn't the type of person to give up easily. When someone knocks you down, you get back up and fight harder. That's what Frenchie had said, but that may have cost him his life.

* * *

Since Washington's traffic seemed to be snarled even at the best of times, Henry decided to take the Metro-rail to RFK stadium and got to the stadium much faster than he expected. Even though it was quite early, there were already more people there than had been at the game in Florida. The local MLS soccer team was called D.C. United and there were numerous concessions open offering their merchandise as well as promotions trying to entice the patrons to purchase season tickets.

Henry headed out into the stands and could see David along with his teammates out on the field stretching. Since David was pretty close to the stands, Henry headed over towards him, waved at him and yelled his name. A security guard was keeping a close eye on Henry.

"It's OK. He's my son," Henry said. David had heard him and come over to see him. David was scanning all of the people in the stands and Henry could tell he was nervous. "Don't be nervous son. You'll do just fine. Just pretend you're playing a game back home at your high school."

Henry gave him a quick hug before he sprinted back over to join his teammates. They went through a few more pre-game drills before they headed back into their dressing room. In the dressing room, most of the players were chattering and buzzing with excitement, but not David. He was sitting in front of his locker with his head down looking like he was about to throw up.

"Anybody using this locker?" someone said as he pulled the locker door open.

"Alex!" David said, rising to give his best friend a hug. "What are you doing here?"

Alex lowered his voice so the rest of the players couldn't hear. "Apparently Tim was mouthing off about being sat down for this game and the coach sent him home. Coach called me last night and said if I could be here by game time, I'd be able to suit up. My dad drove all night to get me here."

"Awesome!" David said, giving him another hug.

"It's no big deal," Alex said. "I'll probably just sit on the bench the whole game." But it was a big deal, and they both knew it.

"Alex," the coach yelled from across the locker-room. "Here's your jersey" he said as he threw it to him.

David was surprised when he saw the disappointed look on Alex's face. "What's the matter?" David asked.

Alex spun the jersey around so that David could read it. "They spelled my name wrong."

They had spelled his name "Bujazcek" instead of "Bujaczek." David was just about to say that no one would notice when he suddenly remembered the sewing kit his Grandma had put in his soccer bag. "I can fix that," David said, grabbing the jersey from Alex.

"OK boys, let's head out to the field," the coach yelled.

"Tell the coach I'll be out in a minute," David said.

The crowd cheered when both teams headed out onto the field. Henry was standing up applauding looking for David, but couldn't locate him and was getting more and more concerned. It was almost five minutes later when he saw David run out onto the field.

"Make sure you exchange your jersey with number 19 after the game," David said to Alex as he handed the jersey to Alex. "It's important." Alex grinned from ear to ear to see his jersey with the correct spelling on it. He held it up and showed it to his father in the stands before he put it on.

Once the game started, it became apparent that this game would have much more intensity than their previous game in Florida. The American team seemed to be spurred on by the crowd and scored a quick goal. But Canada had responded almost immediately with the tying goal. Since then, both teams had numerous good scoring chances. Henry could see the smile on David's face as he played. Even after he had been fouled hard by one of the American players, he continued to flash a smile and it was apparent that he was having the time of his life.

At half-time, Henry stood to stretch his legs and scanned the crowd which had grown fairly large during the first half of play. Suddenly his eyes locked on two men in suits who were sitting about 20 rows behind him. They looked suspiciously like the two men he had seen watching him at the game in Florida.

"This is stupid," Henry thought to himself. "Don't be paranoid. There are a lot of guys wearing suits here today." Sure enough, Henry saw a dozen or more guys in suits scattered throughout the stands. It seemed like they were all wearing sunglasses, but then again, so was he as it was a bright sunny day. Henry saw two more guys in dark suits and sunglasses standing up against the rails at the end of his row. There was a woman talking to one of the men. When she turned, Henry could not believe his eyes. It was Laura.

Henry stood there frozen trying to figure out what was going on. Laura had seen him and started heading down the aisle toward him. "What's going on? Who are those men?"

"Come with me and I'll explain," Laura said.

Henry was in such a state of confusion that he couldn't have resisted even if he wanted to. Laura pulled Henry into one of the exit tunnels where there were no other people. "That's Todd," Laura said. "You know, the FBI agent I was telling you about. I called him today and asked him to keep an eye on you."

"Why?"

"Because something strange is going on and I'm worried that you might be in danger. We found out this morning that the car accident that Frenchie Bouchard was involved in was no accident. Someone tampered with the car. It seems that anyone associated with your brother has a much higher chance of getting into an accident."

"Why didn't you call me?"

"I did, but I didn't get an answer. I thought you might be in trouble so I called Todd. I had to do something."

Henry reached into his pocket and pulled out his cell

phone. Sure enough, it showed that he had five missed calls. "You must have called when I was on the Metro-rail. Are those other guys with the FBI as well?"

"What other guys?" Laura asked.

"The two guys in the grey suits - they're sitting about twenty rows behind me and I thought they were watching me. I think they may have been watching me when I was in Florida as well."

Henry pulled Laura out of the exit tunnel so he could point them out to her, but they were gone. "This is so strange," Henry said. "I have nothing to do with a secret network. Why would anyone think that I did?"

"It's because of your brother. The chatter is that Goliath, which is what you said your brother's code name was, is still active. The NRA is nervous about the vote on the President's gun control legislation which gets voted on tonight in the Senate."

"I'm just here to watch my son's soccer game," Henry said, trying to comprehend the situation.

Carter and Cujo were trying to blend into the crowd outside of the concession stands. They had bolted from their seats shortly after Henry had recognized them. They had also picked out the FBI agent standing at the end of the aisle and decided it was time for them to make their exit. They had called their boss to let him know the situation and once again, dumped the cell phone in a trash can on their way out.

The second half of the game had been going on for a while, although Henry had been oblivious to it. Henry headed back to his seat and Laura sat in the seat beside him. A few minutes later, Todd came over and sat beside Laura. "Hey, Laura," Todd said. "I have to head back to headquarters. I don't think your friend is in any real danger here."

"I'm sorry," Laura said. "I'm probably just being paranoid." Laura realized she had never introduced them. "Henry, this is Todd – Todd, this is my boyfriend Henry."

"Nice to meet you," Henry said as he shook Todd's hand. Todd was younger, better looking and was obviously in very good shape. He looked like he should be featured on brochures to recruit people to join the FBI.

"Nice to meet you sir," Todd said as he removed his sunglasses. He seemed to assess Henry in a single glance. "Make sure you take care of Laura." Henry sensed this was more of a command than a request.

"Thanks so much," Laura said, giving Todd a quick kiss on the cheek. Todd gave a quick signal to his partner who was waiting at the end of the aisle and they headed out of the stadium together.

"I suppose it was silly of me to think that you were in some kind of danger," Laura said, reaching over to take Henry's hand.

"Paranoid behaviour seems to be contagious," Henry said, glancing around to see if the two guys in the grey suits had returned. They hadn't.

Henry turned his focus back to the soccer game just in time to see David streaking down the right side of the field with the ball. He fed a pass into the middle and that player chipped the ball over top of the defender back to David who hadn't broken stride. David hit a perfect cross which was easily headed into the back of the net by one of the Canadian strikers.

The Canadians in the crowd let out a loud cheer. Even the American supporters who were sitting around Henry were commenting about what a nice goal it was, even though it now put the Canadians up 3-2. David celebrated with his teammates and then looked up at Henry as he ran back to get into position. Even though the distance between them was large, their eyes seemed to lock on each other for an instance as if guided by a laser.

It was only a few minutes later when the final whistle was blown. The Canadian team had come through the three friendly matches with a win, a loss and a tie which was much better than expected.

Henry watched as the Canadian players exchanged jerseys with the American players. It was great to see the players from both countries heading off the field together as if they had been friends forever.

*** CHAPTER 25 ***

Henry unfolded the newspaper at breakfast the next day back at home. "Gun Control Legislation Fails in House," read the headline. The story went on to say that the President's new gun control legislation failed to pass in the House of Representatives. The President had announced that he would be addressing the nation at a press conference later that night.

"David will be disappointed," Henry thought to himself. Once again the politicians had spent so much time arguing with each other that they had failed to make any kind of progress. Henry wondered whether David even knew. He would be on the bus with the rest of the team heading back to Canada. It should be a fun bus ride as he knew they would be celebrating their victory over the American team.

When Henry was in the office later that morning, he stopped by Greg Blackwood's office. He was in the process of removing his gun collection from their cases. "I figured it was about time to let these things go," Greg said when he saw Henry.

"I thought you were going to keep a few of them from

your dad's old collection?" Henry said.

"Times have changed and we have to change with them," Greg said. "Sometimes the old ways do more harm than good. You can't use force to get people to do what you want. You just have to reason with people and trust they will do the right thing." Henry sensed that Greg was talking about more than his father's old gun collection.

That evening Henry was watching the hockey game when he heard some good news. At the intermission, the commentators announced that Frenchie Bouchard was now out of intensive care. Although it would be a few more months until he was back on the air, he was expected to make a full recovery.

"Thank God," Henry thought to himself. A few minutes later, the broadcast was interrupted to go to live coverage of the President's press conference.

"Good evening everyone. As you are aware, we failed to obtain the necessary votes yesterday in the House of Representatives to pass the gun control legislation I had put forward. That legislation is effectively dead. However, I believe addressing this issue is critical to the future of our great nation and I refuse to give up."

"Tomorrow morning I will be introducing new legislation for approval in both the Senate and the House of Representatives. I know both parties have been putting forward their ideas for such legislation, but this is not just a watered-down version of my previous proposal with enough compromises to obtain approval. It is completely new legislation with a new approach and new ideas. I'm hopeful that we can allow free votes on this legislation so that we can move forward as a nation."

The President then opened the floor for questions. "Mr. President, since your current legislation just failed to get approval in the House yesterday and you're introducing new legislation so quickly, have you had a task force working on this new legislation behind the scenes knowing your initial proposal was not likely to succeed?"

"No," said the President. "I did not have another task force working on this initiative. This new legislation was just given to me this morning, but I believe this new approach is the correct path forward."

Although they didn't show the faces of the reporters asking the questions, Henry immediately recognized Laura's voice when she asked the next question. "Mr. President, if your task force did not create this new legislation, can you tell us who did?"

The President paused before answering. "No, I can't. To be honest, I'm not sure myself. However, it is apparent that our friends from Canada and England had a hand in putting this proposal together. Although they are not perfect, those two nations don't seem to have a problem with gun violence to the same degree that we have here in the United States. I welcome their ideas and their input."

The President then pointed to a reporter to ask the next question. "Mr. President, why do you think this new legislation will get approval from all parties where the previous legislation failed?"

The President turned his head and gestured for two people who had been standing on the side to join him at the podium. "I'd like to welcome the Majority Leader of the Senate and the Speaker of the House to join me here at the podium. It turns out this new legislation was presented to both of these representatives at the same time it was presented to me and I believe I'm correct in that it will be supported by all parties." The Majority Leader of the Senate and the Speaker of the House both nodded their agreement.

"Mr. President, does this new legislation have the

support of the NRA?"

The President thought carefully before answering. "I believe that's a question the NRA should answer for themselves, but I believe we have the support of both the Democrats and the Republicans and more importantly, I believe we will have the support of the American people. I believe today will be a very important day for the United States of America." The President then thanked everyone for coming and left the podium.

Henry sat stunned by what he had just heard. It was rare to see anything supported by both major parties. Henry wished David had been there to see it.

* * *

The next morning Henry was still in bed when he heard the door-bell. It was early, very early, and Henry laid in bed wondering whether he had actually heard it or just dreamed it. When he heard the pounding on the door, he knew it wasn't a dream. He threw on a robe and was surprised to see detective Benedetti when he opened the door. The expression on the detective's face told him this was not good news.

"We found the plane," the detective said after he stepped into the house. He moved over to sit on the couch. "The plane crashed into the water east of Cornwall," continued the detective. "There were no survivors. I'm so sorry for your loss."

Henry gave a heavy sigh. He thought this day would come eventually but it still came as a shock. "Cornwall?" Henry asked. "Why would they have been so far east?"

"That's why it took us so long to find the plane," said the detective. "It crashed into the water and it has been covered in ice and snow for months. It's only when the ice and snow started melting that it was discovered. We can't say for sure at this point, but we suspect that they lost their instruments and were flying blind in the blizzard that occurred that night." The detective paused before continuing. "We suspect that someone may have tampered with the plane."

* * *

The next few days were extremely hard for the family, especially for Grandma. Kids are never supposed to die before their parents. She was the one who had held out hope that Alan would be found alive. Henry didn't tell her any of the details about the plane crash that had been told him by detective Benedetti, but she sensed that it was Alan's involvement with the secret network that was behind it all. Although Alan had gotten into lots of trouble in his teen years, he had always managed to come out unscathed. It seemed ironic that the single greatest thing he had been involved with in his life would be the thing that did him in.

*** CHAPTER 26 ***

As it normally was, the room was in total darkness except for the glow of light coming from the computer screen. "Please enter your password:" prompted the screen. The complex combination of letters and numbers was carefully entered.

"Welcome, Goliath" flashed on the screen. The cursor scrolled down further and a single ">" prompt appeared.

"Transfer of package successful. Project complete," he typed.

Suddenly the door flew open and light filled the room. "Grandma!" David said. "I'd appreciate it if you'd knock instead of just barging into my room!"

"Sorry," Grandma said. "It's time for supper," she said as she left, leaving the door partially open.

David looked at the prompt on the computer screen and typed "Waiting for next assignment." He closed the laptop and carefully slid it into his soccer bag, under the piece of plastic at the bottom of the bag so it wouldn't come into contact with his sweaty socks and jersey. He picked up the small piece of leather that still sat on the desk, the one with the Goliath name on one side and a weird combination of letters and numbers that was the secret password on the other, and put it into the bag along with the computer. His uncle had tried to teach him the limerick to say to himself to help him remember the password, but David always seemed to forget so he wasn't quite ready yet to get rid of the aid just yet.

David looked at the latest jersey from the American team that he pinned up on his wall. He thought of his best friend Alex who had exchanged his jersey with number 19 from the American team. He knew Alex didn't know that he had sewn the tiny disk into the name on his jersey and he didn't have to know. All David had to say was that it was important to exchange jerseys with a certain player and that was a good enough reason. Best friends are like that.

David had to come up with a new plan when Frenchie had been taken out in the accident. Sewing the disks into suits like his uncle had done was no longer an option. When the old way doesn't work anymore, new ideas are required.

Finally, David looked at the World Cup soccer ball that he had carefully cleaned and polished so it looked like it had never left the box and thought of his Uncle Alan. He remembered the day he had jogged around the track with his uncle and the bizarre request he had made to continue on his work if anything ever happened to him. He was sure that his uncle was just on one of his bipolar fantasy trips so had agreed, but the events that followed convinced him it was no illusion. He remembered rescuing the laptop and hiding it in his soccer bag before their house was broken into.

Uncle Alan had been right. David hadn't killed Goliath with his slingshot like in that old story. Goliath would never die. David had become Goliath.

* * *

The funerals were held about ten days later. Edward Bronson's funeral was covered by the press and attended by hundreds and hundreds of people. Alan's funeral was attended by about twenty people, mostly family and people from the menswear store, and wasn't mentioned at all in the newspaper.

David wore the suit that his uncle had set aside for him for his high school graduation. Robert wore the leather coat that Alan had planned to give to him at Christmas. And Henry wore the last suit he would ever get from his brother.

Henry wrote the eulogy for this brother, with assistance from Laura. Although Henry knew what he wanted to say, he couldn't seem to get it into words without her assistance. As Henry was wrapping up his remarks at the service, he noticed three people sitting at the very back of the church. One was Greg Blackwood. The second was Frenchie Bouchard, although most people wouldn't have recognized him because he wasn't wearing the flashy clothes he normally wore, just a plain black suit. Henry didn't recognize the third man.

Outside the church after the service, Greg and Frenchie came up and offered their condolences to Henry and the other family members. Henry noticed David talking to the third man in the garden area beside the church. They shook hands and then David came over to join the rest of the family.

"Who was that you were talking to in the garden area?" Henry asked David.

"He didn't give his name," David said. "He said he was an associate of Edward Bronson and would be continuing on with Mr. Bronson's legacy. He said he hoped that I would be continuing on with Uncle Alan's legacy."

Henry had never thought of his brother leaving a legacy and wondered what that meant. But David knew exactly what he meant.

Made in the USA
Lexington, KY
12 January 2014